THE PEOPLE IN CONDO 68

THE PEOPLE IN CONDO 68

A Davis Family Sci-Fi Adventure

Robert W. Crumpacker

For Andy

Table of Contents

Acknowledgements

Thanks to Carolyn and Larry McKinney of Portland, Oregon; Alan Hofer of Portland, Oregon; Jeannie Spangler of Davis, California; Larry Armstrong of Borrego Springs, California; Mary Kendrick of Columbus, Indiana; and Barbara and Norman Sepunek of Portland, Oregon for their comments and advice; to my wife, Caroline, for her patience and support; and to the Baileys, Reeds, and Davises for everything else.

1

The Snow Cap Drive In

It was Friday afternoon in mid-July and Caroline and I were driving to Mountainview Ranch, a vacation resort in Central Oregon to visit our grandkids—Clayton Davis, 11, Sam Davis, 9, Mattie Davis, 2—and their mom, Naomi. We would be staying a few days and had been told to arrive at dinnertime.

We lived in Portland, Oregon, the Davises in Hong Kong. The six thousand miles between us made visits difficult and infrequent, but the Davises owned a vacation home at Mountainview Ranch that allowed us to see them summers and winters when they came to visit.

Friday traffic into Central Oregon was usually slow and tedious, but not today. A few miles from the Ranch and it was only four-thirty. We were early. Although we could have chosen to start our visit early, we had a better idea: we'd drive to the Snow Cap Drive In for ice cream. So, ignoring the turn-off to Mountainview Ranch we drove on to the nearby town of Sisters.

Sisters, Oregon is a picture-perfect tourist town built in the Old West style and like many vacation spots, its off and on-season personalities were very different. In winter, Sisters was a sleepy community of two thousand, a place to grab a sandwich and refuel on the way to livelier destinations. But in summer, when all its events and activities were in full swing, Sisters became a vacationer's paradise; its shops, restaurants, and outdoor venues filled with visitors and its streets lined with the same bumper-to-bumper traffic that now separated us from the Snow Cap.

But we were patient and when an opening appeared I popped through it into the Snow Cap's parking lot and within seconds Caroline and I had joined the long line of ice cream lovers shuffling slowly toward the Snow Cap's door.

The Snow Cap Drive In was a Sisters landmark, loved by locals and visitors alike for the heavenly taste of its handmade ice cream. Though city regulations stated that all businesses must be built in the Old West style, the Snow Cap had been wisely excused from that requirement to be what it's always been: a small, dumpy, white box serving ice cream as good as any on the planet.

Our progress continued until at last we held two magnificent waffle cones, Caroline's heaped with marionberry ice cream and mine with Oreo and peanut butter parfait. By the time we'd returned to Mountainview Ranch the cones were gone, leaving a trail of delicious memories in their wake.

Entering the Ranch, we stopped at the little office just inside the property for a parking pass and a magnetic swipe card that would allow us to move freely throughout the resort, then wound down Central Drive to the long row of Country House Condominiums. The Davises' condo was one of the last, so at the final cluster of buildings we turned left into the lot and parked. We grabbed our stuff, tromped across the noisy wooden walkway to Country House Condominium number 64, and walked in.

2

Golf Balls

nside, the furniture, pictures, and decorations were all familiar and the place had the same worn and comfortable feel it always had, but it was different. The reason for this was the golf balls. There were golf balls everywhere, the Davis kids in their midst. They barely glanced at us as we put our bags down.

"Hi, guys," I said, "Great to be here. Great to see you."

Caroline added her greetings, but we didn't get much of a reception. Clayton and Sam left the balls long enough to give us distracted hugs then returned to their tasks. Mattie, red-framed sunglasses atop her head, smiled faintly in our direction and continued arranging balls in a long, winding row on the floor.

Though Mattie's project was clearly artistic, what the boys were doing was less obvious. As I watched them some more it appeared that much of their work involved sorting. The boys had surrounded themselves with several bowls and pans and seemed to be separating the balls based upon their condition: some containers for the better balls and other containers for the rest.

And balls were being counted and stored. Beyond the bowls and pans lay a row of soiled pillowcases, each partially filled with golf balls. The pillowcases' outlying position suggested that they were the balls' final stop and as the balls were transferred from the bowls and pans to the pillowcases they were counted, their numbers called out and recorded on scraps of paper.

And all balls were marked with patches of red paint, identifying them as driving range balls.

This work, whatever it was, was not done quietly. There was a lot of "Not a good ball, Dude," and "Dude, it goes here! Really, Dude, I'm serious!" and "Dude, we've counted those before so they go in the pillowcase!" and rarely, "Oh, no, Dude, we messed up! Better count them again."

And finally, I tried connecting the balls to their condo's location. Behind the Country House Condominiums was a huge expanse of thick green grass that gave the kids nearly unlimited space to run and play. Beyond the lawn was a wild, untended stretch of dry earth, scrub grass, and short thorny bushes that extended back another fifty yards and ended at a high fence separating the owners' property from the resort's driving range, which, I suspected, was where the balls had originated.

Then I glanced through the sliding glass doors at the rear of their house. Though I had seen that view countless times before, it never failed to amaze me. To the left of the driving range was a lake for fishing and boating and a grassy meadow for the riding horses; behind the meadow, lake, and driving range the vacation homes were sprinkled through a dark green forest of ponderosa pines; and above everything stood the snow-capped peaks of the Three Sisters, Broken Top, and Mount Washington; the spectacular mountain vista for which the ranch was named.

Just then the kids' mom, Naomi, walked around the wall separating the kitchen from the eating area, and more recently, the golf balls. Naomi was a handsome woman; tall, fit and tan with long straight dark hair. Her ancestry was Irish-American on her mother's side and Samoan on her father's. The result of this blend gave Naomi a strong, exotic beauty. Besides being attractive, she was smart, tough, and had a wonderful sense of humor. And, she was a great mom. Our son, Tris—short for Tristan—had been living right the day he found her. Naomi hugged us, welcomed us to the Ranch, and apologized for the golf balls.

"Naomi," I said, "It's great being here, but you've got to tell us about the balls. What's going on?"

Naomi laughed. "What you're seeing is Central Oregon's newest and most successful business. The boys are selling driving range balls back to the golf shop and in a few days they'll have more money than all the adults at Mountainview put together." She laughed again.

"The golf shop pays a dollar for every hundred usable balls that the kids collect in the area between the lawn and the fence, and there are a lot of balls out there. The machine that picks them up stays inside the fence and either it's too easy for balls to get past the fence or no one's ever picked them up there before. But whatever the reason, it's been good for everyone."

"Mom!" complained Mattie.

"Oh, I'm sorry, honey," said Naomi, "I forgot you, didn't I? Then there's Mattie. While Clayton and Sam are only interested in the money, Mattie wants to make beautiful golf ball designs for everyone to enjoy. And, she collects the balls, too."

Naomi looked proudly at her kids. "And they've made six or seven dollars in just the last three days."

"SORRY MOM, BUT YOU'RE WRONG AGAIN!" said Sam in a loud, authoritative voice; "WE'VE EARNED TEN DOLLARS and right now we have OVER THREE HUNDRED BALLS to take to the shop tomorrow! YES FRIENDS," he announced, flashing an impish smile, "THE BIG MONEY'S ROLLIN' IN!"

"Well, Mr. BIG businessman," Naomi said, smiling but serious, "I'll remind you that your business must be outside on the deck in fifteen minutes, and after dinner you and Clayton need to pack up all the balls so you can take them to the golf shop first thing in the morning. And Mattie, I want you to give your balls to the boys, too."

A worried Mattie looked up at Naomi.

"It's okay, Mattie," Naomi assured her, "They'll be more balls tomorrow. I promise."

The boys moved the balls out onto the deck then we talked about school, sports, and golf balls while Caroline presented Mattie with a brand new pair of sparkly blue-framed sunglasses.

Soon, Naomi called us to dinner and, as always, served a delicious and healthy dinner, low in fat and sugar, and high in nutrition. Most of the foods were organic and there were bowls of fresh fruits and vegetables in the middle of the table for everyone to pick from.

After dinner Caroline and I helped with the dishes while the boys finished sorting the balls and packing them into pillowcases for tomorrow's big payday. We talked for a while but it had been a busy day and everyone was tired. Mattie went to bed first, the boys followed, and the adults brought up the rear. Caroline and I said goodnight to Naomi and climbed the narrow stairs to our bedroom on the second floor.

Beside our bed was a photograph of the kids that I never tired of looking at. On the left was Clayton; long, dark brown hair, olive skin, and soulful brown eyes set in a broad, heart-shaped face. He was looking into the camera with a solemn expression that was warm, open, and honest.

Sam was on the right. Though two years younger than his brother, he was already the taller of the two boys. Sam's face was longer than Clayton's, his features more prominent, and his coloring lighter. Sam had turned from the camera but continued watching it, a devilish grin on his lips and his blue eyes filled with mischief.

Between the boys stood little Mattie, looking fearlessly into the camera, her face a softer version of Clayton's, her merry blue eyes a more innocent version of Sam's.

Clayton was holding a soccer ball. Though all three kids loved sports, Clayton had poured all his energy into soccer and could spend days on end reading about it, watching it, and practicing it. Sam played soccer, too, but his interests extended to other areas, especially math and science. Sam was also the family comic, but beneath the humor was a bright, inquisitive mind that could startle you with its insight.

Though not yet three, Mattie loved soccer every bit as much as the boys, and could kick a soccer ball with frightening abandon. Running, her blond hair often flew into her face, but she had mastered the technique of flattening her upper lip and blowing the hair away, only adding to her look of single-minded fury.

But Mattie's trademark was her sunglasses, and when she wasn't wearing them indoors and out, they were positioned in readiness on top of her head.

Caroline and I unpacked and crawled into bed. Happy and looking forward to the next few days, I kissed her goodnight and fell into a dreamless sleep.

3

A Bump In The Night

But suddenly and without knowing why, I found myself awake. At first, I thought that Caroline had bumped me, but when I looked at her she was in exactly the same position she'd been in when we'd said goodnight.

As strange as the idea seemed, it felt like the bed had been lifted and dropped. But what would cause something like that? An earthquake? I didn't think so. I'd been in a couple of earthquakes and both times there had been a series of jolts, not just one.

I looked at my watch. It was 2:30 a.m. I listened. It was quiet. I looked out the picture window across from the foot of the bed; the moon and stars were bright and the sky was clear. Unable to find an explanation, I turned over and went back to sleep.

Next morning, Caroline was still asleep when I rolled out of bed. Standing, I remembered last night's awakening, but with no fresh ideas as to its cause I pushed it from my mind, threw on some shorts, brushed my teeth, shaved, and went downstairs for breakfast.

Naomi was in the kitchen and updated me on the kids' activities: Mattie was still in bed but Clayton and Sam had been up for a couple of hours and had already delivered their golf balls to the pro shop. Due to a counting error they'd made four dollars instead of three, and encouraged by their unexpected success they were back outside collecting more balls.

I ate some breakfast then went out to see what the boys were up to. At first I couldn't find them, but then I spotted them in the distance, working the far area between the lake and fence.

When I reached them I announced I was there to work but would first need some instruction. I was told that the job right now was simply to collect every golf ball, both good and bad, that I could find.

Surprised, I asked why it was necessary to collect the bad balls and was given two reasons. First, balls were sometimes so coated with dirt and dust that their exact condition was a mystery until after they'd been cleaned. And second, if bad balls were left on the ground they would slow and confuse all future searches for good balls. It was best to start clean.

Though it was a more complicated explanation than I expected, it made a lot of sense. I nodded and got to work.

It didn't take me long to realize the truth of what Naomi had told us last night: there were a lot of balls out here.In fact, golf balls must have been accumulating beyond the fence for as long as the driving range had been there. The balls were of all ages and those that had survived more than a winter or two were often in pretty bad shape.

The boys were working the area outside the fence in a careful and logical manner. They had started above the lake at the far end of the driving range and were gradually moving counter-clockwise around the fence toward the Country Home Condominiums. Eventually they would be working near their own backyard.

It was hard work and after a couple of hours I was tired and my back hurt. Being shorter and younger would have helped, but satisfied that I had made a contribution, I excused myself and returned to the house.

That turned out to be an excellent decision. Naomi had just finished making some yummy scones and Mattie was up and looking for someone to entertain her. Being the newest member of the family, I didn't know Mattie as well as I did the boys, but I soon discovered that she was very skilled at picking good books for me to read, positioning herself comfortably on my lap, and escaping capture when I suddenly became a monster with an appetite for little girls.

4

Some Kind Of Something

The day passed enjoyably. To Mattie's delight, Caroline finally came downstairs. The boys broke for lunch. A rest time followed lunch, then a soccer game on the lawn, more golf ball work, and finally another tasty and nutritious dinner.

The golf ball processing plant had been permanently moved to the deck, so after dinner the boys went outside and sorted the day's catch. Using a space between two boards, Mattie had created a spectacular row of balls running the entire length of the deck.

Then Naomi stuck her head out and told the kids to wrap it up for the night. I sat in the waning sunlight reading as Mattie gave her balls to the boys, who counted them and made the final transfer of balls to pillowcases. At last count they had collected over three hundred good balls. In fact, they needed only eleven more to make it four hundred.

The boys ran inside and begged Naomi for permission to collect more balls. She said no, but they pleaded their case: eleven balls would make it four hundred, tying their all-time record.

"Please, mom, just a little longer!"

At first, Naomi wouldn't bend; they had to finish now and could get the extra balls in the morning. But the boys persisted. "Please, mom, please! It won't take long. Please, mom."

The boys were persuasive and Naomi was firm but not rigid. Finally, she told them to take the yellow flashlight from the closet, find eleven more good balls and come right back in. The boys promised and after an excited clamor of running feet and slamming doors they were back outside with a fresh bucket, the yellow flashlight blazing.

We sat inside, happily awaiting their next burst of infectious enthusiasm, but the night got quiet and the boys were slow to return. Curious, I glanced outside but could see them in the scrub area behind the lawn, their flashlight pointed at the ground. Everything seemed okay.

Ten or fifteen minutes later we heard slow footsteps on the deck. The screen door slid open and the boys entered the room. They looked at us, then at each other, then at us again. They weren't smiling.

Naomi said, "Did you get the balls?"

There was a pause. They looked at each other again.

Clayton answered. "We got some of them."

Another pause.

"They were hard to see in the dark," added Sam.

"You were out there quite a while," Naomi said. "We saw the flashlight. It seemed to be working all right."

Another pause. More looks. Then Clayton said, "There was something out there."

Naomi looked at the boys. "What was out there?"

"It was weird," said Clayton.

"YEAH," agreed Sam, "WEIRD AND SCARY TOO!"

That got our attention.

"Was it an animal?" Caroline asked.

Another pause.

"No, it was something else," said Clayton, taking a deep breath. "At least it didn't look like an animal."

Then slowly and deliberately pinning him with her eyes, Naomi said, "Clayton, would you please tell us what you saw?"

Clayton looked at the floor for a long time then lifted his head and stammered, "Well…it was round…and kind of big."

"How big was it?" Naomi said.

Sam answered first. "It was about as long as we are tall but not as high," he said. "It was round but looked soft, like a ball that doesn't have enough air or a giant water balloon laying on the ground."

"And we could see through it," said Clayton.

"Yeah, and there was stuff inside," Sam added.

Though it was cool I had begun to perspire.

Then in a voice so loud it startled me, Sam bellowed, "LET'S GO LOOK AT IT!"

But no one jumped up to follow his suggestion.

"Did you touch it?" I asked.

"We were going to touch it," Sam answered, "but then we didn't."

"Good!" chorused the adults.

"Was it moving?" I asked.

Clayton and Sam looked at each other as though there might be a problem answering that correctly.

Finally Clayton said, "Well, not on the outside, but it was moving on the inside."

"No," Sam added, "It wasn't going anywhere, but it was sort of swirling inside."

That produced another silence then Mattie began to fuss. I glanced at my watch. It was late, past her bedtime.

Then, something unexpected happened. In a clear, steady voice I said, "I'll go look at it," and as soon as the words had left my mouth I felt relaxed and in control.

"Naomi," I said, "you can put Mattie to bed. I saw where the boys were standing. They're fine, so I'll be okay. I'll see what it is then we can talk about it."

For me, this was unusual behavior. I was rarely the first to do anything, especially if it involved danger. I was a good follower, a faithful helper. So, I'm not sure why I volunteered. My best guess is that at that moment my curiosity had simply overcome my fear.

I said goodnight to Mattie, reached for the flashlight, and walked out the door. As I entered the darkness beyond the house, I briefly regretted not having left in a more dramatic fashion, but at that moment additional drama seemed unnecessary.

5

The Thing

The dry evening air warmed my skin. A faint pink outlined the mountains but the landscape was otherwise dark and featureless. Glad for the flashlight, I walked steadily across the lawn but slowed at the border between the grass and the drier area beyond. I was very close to where I had seen the boys standing. The thing, whatever it was, wasn't far away.

As I moved from the cool grass to the warm, dusty earth, I realized I wasn't wearing shoes and suddenly felt exposed and vulnerable. But I wasn't stopping. I continued forward, though more slowly, my flashlight pointed at the ground.

Then, ten or fifteen feet in front of me the flashlight's beam reflected off something smooth and shiny, and in the dry, dusty area I was crossing anything "smooth and shiny" was definitely out of place. It was the thing. I kept moving until I was five or six feet away from it. Then I stopped.

I studied it carefully before going any closer. At first, what I saw reminded me of a jellyfish that had washed up on the beach, but was much, much larger. In fact, its size was about what Clayton and Sam had said it was: about four feet across and two feet above the ground. It appeared to be resting in a depression and didn't look like it was going anywhere.

Feeling safer, I continued inching forward until I was a foot or two away and from there I leaned over and pointed the flashlight down onto it. Its skin or shell or whatever its outer coat was looked thick but elastic, giving it the deflated-ball or water-balloon-on-the-ground appearance that the boys had described. Its skin was dusty but transparent and what I saw inside surprised me so much I heard myself gasp. Inside its outer shell were many smaller balls, each containing a clear, thick, reddish liquid in which small particles of various colors were suspended and were moving, rotating, all at the same slow speed.

What I saw was so strange and beautiful that for a few seconds I forgot to be afraid. I'd never seen anything like it. Although I knew it was a crazy conclusion to draw after so brief a look, my first thought was that whatever this thing was it came from someplace besides Earth. Then, with a start, I remembered last night's awakening and wondered, "Could this thing, falling from the sky, have made the jolt that woke me up?"

And I knew it could.

6

Back Home

I have no memory of walking back to the house or going inside. But when my mind finally came back from wherever it had been, everyone except Mattie was sitting at the dinner table, staring at me. I tried to speak but couldn't, my mouth felt like it had been stuffed with cotton.

After several seconds I tried again and this time I was able to say, "Saw it," in a raspy whisper. I kept clearing my throat and licking my lips trying to produce a little spit, but eventually gave up and just kept rasping.

"Sorry...for voice. Like boys said....giant water balloon...four feet across...clear outside...smaller balls inside....stuff moving around...not going anywhere."

With those few words I had told them nothing more than what Clayton and Sam had already described. Although I should have mentioned last night's bump, at that moment additional speech was beyond my ability.

Thankfully, Caroline had heard enough. "So, what should we do?" she asked matter-of-factly.

Although I might have tried listing our choices, I thought that everyone, the kids included, knew what they were: we could call the police now or call them in the morning.

Of course, the smart choice would have been to call them now, but if the police were called now they would arrive with flashlights blazing, cameras flashing, asking endless questions, and eventually calling for a lift-truck to haul the thing away; all of which would keep the neighborhood awake and on edge the rest of the night. No, I thought, dealing with it tonight would be a mess.

I was also aware of just how tired I felt and as I glanced around the table, everyone there looked equally weary.

Then, as if reading my mind, Naomi said, "Of course we should call the police, but could it wait until tomorrow?"

Whatever the thing was, it didn't look like it was going anywhere.

"Yes," I answered hoarsely, "I think it could."

Naomi stood. "Okay," she said, "unless I hear an objection in the next ten seconds, we're all going to bed."

No one said a word.

"Then it's settled," she said firmly, "I'll call the police first thing in the morning and let them handle it. We'll be fine. Boys, don't forget to brush your teeth."

Naomi walked to the sliding glass doors and locked them, but left the blinds open so the inside lights would cast a visible perimeter around the back of the house. Everything seemed settled. I picked up my book and started for the stairs, hoping we were doing the right thing.

Caroline and I went right to bed and Caroline fell asleep instantly. I fell asleep, too, but it wasn't a restful sleep. Almost immediately I began dreaming and in my dream I saw the smaller balls, their insides at first moving lazily just as they had done outside. But then the pace of their movement increased and soon the bags themselves were rotating, their speed gradually increasing until they were spinning like high-speed drills, boring through the outer container, spilling out onto the lawn, and wiggling toward the house. I woke in a sweaty panic.

Returning to sleep, I found the same unpleasant dream still looping through my brain. This continued until I finally looked at my watch and saw that once again it was 2:30 a.m. Lying in bed with my mind churning like the stuff inside the balls, I wondered if it might make more sense to just go downstairs and take one last look at the thing. If nothing about it had changed maybe I would find that reassuring enough to sleep without dreaming that awful dream. I lay there working up my courage then slipped out of bed, pulled on my shorts, and went downstairs.

As I passed the pile of footwear by the front door, I stopped to put on my shoes. This time I wasn't going out there barefoot. I crossed the floor, took the flashlight from the dining room table, and reached for the lock on the glass doors.

"Bob," said a voice behind me. I nearly fainted. I turned and saw Naomi, fully dressed. She gave a little laugh and said, "Sorry if I scared you, but I'm going, too."

That was good news. I hadn't been looking forward to another trip out there alone.

"Are you ready?" I asked.

"I am," she said. "Let's go."

I opened the doors and we stepped out into the clear, cool night. I switched on the flashlight but the light from the moon and stars was so bright that additional light seemed unnecessary. In fact, as we walked across the lawn I thought I could see the sky's light reflecting off our visitor's dome, and after a few more steps I was sure of it. I stopped and pointed.

"Naomi," I whispered, "Look there! Can you see the light shining off its top?"

"I see *something* shiny," she said, "is that it?"

"Yeah, that's it."

Moving from grass to dirt we barely slowed, but a few feet away from it we stopped. The flashlight combined with the night's natural light filled the thing with an unearthly glow, as though it were somehow illuminated from within. I could now see past the balls on the surface to the balls in the layers below, the contents of each moving in its own direction but at the same slow speed. In a creepy, psychedelic way, it was very beautiful.

Time passed and finally Naomi whispered, "I've seen enough. I'm going back."

I was still so hypnotized that I was slow to respond, but eventually I nodded and we turned toward the house. But then I stopped.

I had seen so much movement inside the little balls that once again I had begun to wonder if somehow the thing might be capable of moving across the ground. As unlikely as that seemed, I had thought of an easy way to test it.

"Wait a second, Naomi," I said, "I want to do one more thing before we go inside."

I played the flashlight across the ground, looking for something to use as a marker. A few feet away I saw a large, diamond-shaped rock that I retrieved and placed about a foot from the thing's left side. Satisfied, I joined Naomi and we began walking toward the house.

But as I stepped from the dry area onto the lawn, I felt that strange sensation you sometimes get when someone unseen is watching you, and when I looked up and to the left, there he was. Seen only in silhouette, a man was standing quietly behind an upstairs window, watching us. The room's light was behind him so he appeared only as a dark shape, his features indistinct. I glanced over at Naomi who was walking to my left, her eyes fixed on the ground. She hadn't seen him and though I was momentarily tempted to say something, I didn't.

7

Wildflowers

Next morning everyone was up early. As Caroline and I entered the dining area, Mattie and the boys were in the living room playing video games and Naomi was just getting off the phone. I walked into the kitchen, poured myself some coffee and saw a do-it-yourself breakfast smorgasbord with a variety of juices, fruits, breads, and cereals spread out across the counter.

"I just finished talking with Officer Justice," said Naomi, smiling.

"Officer Justice? Really?" Caroline said, "What a great name for a policeman."

"Actually Officer Justice is a she," said Naomi, "and she's coming right over."

Caroline and I grabbed some food and a few minutes later there was a knock at the front door. Naomi answered it and returned with a tall, thin young woman wearing aviator sunglasses, the two-tone green uniform of the Mountainview Police Department, and a pair of well-worn cowboy boots. She removed her cap and sunglasses and introduced herself as Officer Sally Justice, and flashing a friendly smile told us to call her Officer Sally or just Sally, then went around the room shaking hands.

When Sally got to Clayton and Sam she squatted down and said, "I bet you're the boys who found that thing last night. Your mom said you were both real brave and your description was right on the mark. So, which one of you is Clayton and which is Sam?"

The boys identified themselves and gave Sally an excited account of last night's discovery. Every so often she would nod and comment, "Nice work," or "Glad you noticed that," and occasionally scribble something in her notebook. At first I was surprised how comfortable Sally and the boys were with each other until I realized that the first requirement for being a law officer at Mountainview Ranch would be getting along well with kids.

Then Officer Sally thanked the boys, stood, and announced, "Well, the boys here just gave me a real good description of the object, so if someone would point me in the right direction, I'll go out and have a look at it myself."

I opened the sliding glass doors and gave her the direction and the thing's approximate location along that line. Sally thanked me and marched across the deck and over the lawn, kicking up dew as she went. We stood at the windows, watching. She was right on course, but when she got to where it should have been, she slowed, stopped, and began to look around. Then she took a few steps back, stopped, and rotated through a full circle, her eyes searching the ground. She hadn't seen it.

I watched until I couldn't stand it any longer then opened the screen door and trotted across the deck, down the stairs, and over the lawn. When I reached the diamond-shaped rock I had placed beside it last night, it wasn't there. Startled, I stepped back to get a wider view, and when I still couldn't see it, I stepped back even further and looked again. As big as the thing had been it should have been easy to see, but nothing caught my eye.

I went back to where it once had been and looked to the right of the diamond-shaped rock. A patch of colorful wildflowers now occupied its spot. What was going on?

"Sally," I said, pointing at the flowers, "it was right there where those flowers are now. I put that rock about a foot to its left so I would know where it had been just in case it moved."

Then I noticed something odd. I bent down and traced my fingers along the front edge of the wildflowers.

"Sally," I said, "look in front of the flowers and tell me what you see."

What I had seen was a slight but noticeable difference in the appearance of the soil surrounding the flowers that began about two or three inches in front of them and extended all the way around. She saw it right away.

"The ground looks different around the flowers than it does a little farther out," she said.

"Now feel it," I said.

Sally put her fingers in the dirt near the flowers and drew them toward her.

"It feels like there's some kind of ledge there," she said. "Close to the flowers the dirt is loose and soft but when I move my hand back, the ground suddenly gets firm, like there's some kind of shoveled-out place where the dirt and flowers have been planted."

She walked around the wildflowers, trailing her hand in the dirt. When she had circled the flowers completely, she stopped and straightened, looking down at the plot.

"That ledge goes all the way around the flowers," she said, "and if you stand back and look at its size and shape, it's about four feet across and round, just like what you, Missus Davis, and the boys saw there last night."

"And Sally," I said, "last night it looked like the thing was lying in a depression that had been created when it hit the ground…like it landed with so much force that it had dented the earth. What we're feeling could be the edge of that dent."

"Well," she said slowly, "that would fit. But if that thing was here last night, where did it go? Did it just get up and leave or did someone haul it away? Either way, you'd expect the dirt around those flowers to be all messed up, but instead the ground's perfectly smooth. And then there're those crazy flowers. Now how in the world could they have gotten planted there so fast?"

I didn't know.

"It doesn't make sense," she said.

I agreed.

We walked around the area a little longer then went back to the house. Naomi met us at the door.

"It wasn't there, was it?" she said.

Sally took a deep breath. "No, Missus Davis, we didn't see it. But something's definitely been there 'cause there's this big, round dent in the ground that's about the same size and shape as what you and the boys saw there last night. But all that's there now is this big patch of wildflowers."

"Wildflowers!" was Naomi's surprised response.

"It's not there?" said Clayton in complete disbelief. "But, Sally, it was there." He looked close to tears. "We saw it, Sally, we really did!"

"Now, Clayton," Sally said, "It's not your fault we didn't see it. In a little bit I'll go out again and you and Sam can help me look. Maybe we just missed it."

But finding no comfort in her words, Clayton threw himself facedown onto an overstuffed chair and pulled a pillow over his head. Sam remained standing, looking up at Officer Justice, an uncertain smile on his face.

"Officer Sally," he said softly, "Do you really believe we saw it?"

"Now, boys," said Sally, exasperated, "I'm sorry that we couldn't find it, but that doesn't mean I don't believe you. Of course I believe you. Not only did you boys see it, but your mom saw it and your granddad did, too. So it was there. But right now all that's there are those crazy flowers."

"And those flowers," I said, "had to have just been planted. If they'd been under that thing last night they'd have been crushed flat. Instead, they're perfect."

"I'll bet someone planted them there to hide the spot where the thing landed," said Caroline.

"And what we saw last night would weigh a lot; two or three hundred pounds, maybe more," Naomi added. "One person couldn't move it."

"I hear you, folks," said Sally, "and I agree with everything you're sayin'. But when we looked around those flowers there was no sign that it had been dragged out of there or had crawled away on its own. Either way there should've been some pretty obvious tracks, but the ground was perfectly smooth."

Sally sighed and pushed her hat back. "Well, I'm not done yet. I'm gonna take another look out there and you're all welcome to join me."

At her invitation, everyone stood, filed into the back yard, and began searching. But one by one we accepted defeat and returned to the house until only Caroline and Sally remained.

Caroline was on her hands and knees, looking intently at the new wildflowers. She pulled some from the ground, shook off the dirt and smelled them, then carried them to the deck where she put them on the picnic table, sat down, and began examining them some more.

Meanwhile, Sally was walking systematically back and forth over a large section of the field as though mowing it with an imaginary lawn mower, her eyes scanning the ground. But after combing the area thoroughly, she returned to the house, shaking her head in frustration.

"Now I looked pretty darn hard out there and didn't see much of anything, except for golf balls. If you boys are interested in making more money, looks like there's still plenty to be made, but whatever else was out there last night looks like it's gone."

We thanked Sally for coming but couldn't hide our disappointment. She handed me her business card and told us to call if we found anything related to the missing bag. Sally promised to discuss the case with the other officers—they'd all been here longer than she had—and maybe one or two of them had seen or heard of something similar. She'd also get their ideas on what should be done next, and promised to call when she had more information. I thanked her again and stuck the card in my wallet.

Sally left and the boys came into the living room, slouched down on the couch, and began talking. After awhile they ran out the back door with Mattie close behind.

Then I had an idea. I walked back out to the wildflowers, turned toward the house, and looked up and to the left, trying to find the window where I'd seen the man standing last night. I thought I recognized the window but couldn't be sure. Counting from our condo, which was number sixty-four, the unit I most suspected was number sixty-eight.

8

My Newest Best Friend

I wasn't sure what to do next. The events of the last two days called for action, but what that action should be I didn't have a clue. Maybe, I thought, doing nothing was an acceptable alternative. After all, strange things had been happening so fast that even if I did nothing then more strange things were sure to happen and eventually we'd have enough information to understand what was going on. It wasn't a very satisfying approach, but at that moment I was all out of better ideas. So, I served myself some more breakfast and sat down to eat and read my book.

But everyone else was taking a more active approach. The kids had been outside walking around and talking for almost an hour when I heard them tromp up the stairs and onto the deck. I looked outside and saw Sam and Mattie stop where Caroline was sitting and pull up chairs beside her.

Clayton continued into the house to the kitchen where Naomi was washing dishes and storing leftovers. I heard him tell her he needed some exercise and asked if he could ride his bike. Clayton loved all forms of physical activity and Naomi was as much an advocate of exercise as she was of sound diet, so it was no surprise when she said yes. Clayton promised to be careful and stay on the bike paths, then ran to the front door, grabbed his bike helmet and hurried outside, the screen door banging shut behind him.

Around eleven-thirty, just as I was beginning to think about lunch, there was a knock at the front door. I went to answer it and there stood a neatly dressed man smiling pleasantly back at me. He looked about forty and was of average height and build; his hair was dark and neatly combed; and he was clean-shaven, his skin tan and unlined. In short, he was one of the most ordinary-looking people I had ever seen. Even his clothes—gray slacks, a black sport shirt, and tasseled black loafers—were such standard-issue resort wear that he almost didn't look real, more like a mannequin that had just stepped out of an L.L. Bean catalog. I waited, thinking that any second he would try to sell me a set of encyclopedias or a life insurance policy, but he just stood there smiling.

Finally I said, "Yes?"

"Good morning," he answered cheerfully, "my name is George Brown and it's very nice to meet you. My family lives over there," he said, waving toward the condos with the bigger numbers, "and as I was walking through the parking lot this morning I saw a set of golf clubs in your car and thought you would enjoy playing golf with me this afternoon. So I called the clubhouse and reserved us a starting time. I will pay for everything and you may even eat lunch at our house."

I was dumbfounded. It was the oddest introduction to another human being I had ever heard. I stared at him speechless, trying desperately to think of something to say that would prevent me from playing golf with him, but as I searched my brain for a believable lie, George continued looking at me and smiling his superpleasant smile. The situation was so bizarre that my mind went blank. He had me.

"Okay," I said reluctantly, "I'll play golf with you, George Brown. My name's Bob Davis and it's nice to meet you, too. And this afternoon's fine. I'll just change my clothes, grab my stuff, and meet you at your condo in a few minutes."

Then I paused trying to remember something else he must have told me, but if he had I'd already forgotten it.

"I'm sorry, George," I said, "what did you say your condo's number was?"

"I don't think I told you that, Bob," he said, still smiling, "but it's number sixty-eight."

Number sixty-eight? My jaw must have dropped a foot, but George's expression didn't change.

"Good," he said, "your lunch will be ready when you arrive and after you've eaten I will drive us to the golf course. It's nice meeting you, Bob. I'm looking forward to our game."

George turned and walked briskly up the boardwalk toward condominium number sixty-eight and I just stood there, frozen to the spot. As soon as George had told me his condo number, I knew exactly who he was: he was the man watching us from the window.

As George's footsteps receded into the distance, I wondered what new weirdness I had just gotten myself into. Although I hoped it was nothing more than two neighbors playing a round of golf, I had my doubts.

I stood there for several minutes, trying to understand what George's presence in the window might have meant and found I could explain it in two very different ways.

The first was to say, "So what if he looked outside and saw us, what's so strange about that?"

I imagined that possibility happening like this: George had had trouble sleeping and was sitting by the window, reading a book and occasionally looking out at the beautiful night sky. Either seeing us or hearing us, he had stood to find out what we were doing and had seen Naomi and I pointing a flashlight at the ground, talking to each other, and moving rocks around. In this case our behavior was stranger than George's.

But seen the other way, George Brown's presence in the window was just one more odd event in a whole series of unusual things that had been happening since we arrived two days ago. And that wasn't all. Sure, George looked like your typical vacationer, but at the same time he looked almost too typical to be real. And how strange was it that he had asked me to play golf after noticing my golf clubs in our car and then offering me a free round of golf and a free lunch? Now, that was strange.

Then there was his speech. Other than the information his words carried, his speech said absolutely nothing about him. He had no accent, used no slang expressions, and made no unusual word choices; his diction and grammar were perfect. A person's speech often says a lot about him, but George's speech was just as unrevealing as the rest of him.

But maybe I was being too hard on the poor guy. Maybe he was new to Mountainview and just looking for someone to play golf with, and although I couldn't quite shake the feeling that there was something very odd about George, I decided to give him the benefit of the doubt.

9

Snow Cones

Although I still had questions about George I had no questions about golf. I liked it and was eager to play. Besides needing a break from the craziness of the last two days, I *had* brought my clubs to Mountainview hoping to play and now that was about to happen. And it was going to be free. I liked that, too. The truth is I'm a little cheap.

I changed into an acceptable golf outfit and told Caroline and Naomi that I'd be playing golf with a neighbor. Then I got my clubs and golf shoes from the car and walked up the boardwalk to number sixty-eight, the home of my newest best friend and soon-to-be golfing buddy, George Brown.

I had just raised my hand to knock, when a smiling young woman who could have been George Brown's sister, opened the door. She didn't look exactly like George—she was blond and blue-eyed—but she had the same smooth good looks that George had. She introduced herself as George's wife and told me to call her Linda. At her invitation I entered their home just as George and a young boy were walking up to greet me.

The boy was more or less a miniature version of George and Linda, a very average-looking kid with George's dark brown hair and regular features. He was wearing a bright green University of Oregon T-shirt with a big yellow "O" in the center. I thought he was about eight or nine. George introduced him as their son, Charles, and I shook his hand.

As I studied the boy some more, I noticed that he had several characteristics that his parents didn't have. For one thing he wasn't smiling all the time. He looked more serious and less out-going than his parents, and as I watched him some more there was something about him that I found appealing. Although I couldn't say what that "something" was, he seemed like the kind of kid who might get along well with our grandchildren.

Then the Browns asked me to join them in the dining room. A full meal was waiting for me on the table, but there were no places set for anyone else. Maybe, I thought, they hadn't had time to set the other places, so I decided to wait until they had, but after a couple of minutes of waiting I began to suspect I was eating alone. I looked inquiringly at the Browns, who were still smiling their identical smiles, and after an uncomfortable pause a look of understanding crossed George's face.

"Oh, I'm sorry, Bob," he said, "please forgive me. I should have told you that we've already eaten. But go ahead and enjoy your lunch and while you're eating we'll have our snow cones. We love snow cones."

Had I heard him correctly? They were having snow cones for lunch? I'd never heard of that before, but maybe the Browns were from some part of the country where eating snow cones at the noon meal was more common than it was in Oregon.

At least my lunch looked good. Linda had fixed me a sliced turkey sandwich with lettuce, mayonnaise, pickles, tomatoes, mustard, and Swiss cheese, served on a thick, toasted, nutritious-looking whole grain bread, with chips and iced tea on the side; it was definitely my kind of lunch. George and Charles sat down and I began eating.

Linda disappeared into the kitchen and I soon heard a mixture of whirring and grinding coming from the family snow cone maker. After a minute or two the noises stopped and Linda entered the room carrying three large red snow cones. She handed cones to George and Charles then took the last one herself and sat down.

It was a good lunch and the Browns were nice hosts. The snow cones seemed odd, but after the last two days I was getting very used to odd.

As soon as I'd finished, George said, "I'm sorry Bob, but we should go now; our tee time is in a few minutes." And with that he stood, gathered his golf equipment, and headed for the door.

George was clearly a man of action, so I quickly thanked Linda for a nice lunch, said good-bye to Charles, grabbed my stuff and followed George out the door for our round of golf.

10

A Game Of Golf

I'm not a very good golfer but I still like to play. In fact, I probably would have played without all the incentives that George had offered me, but the incentives were nice, too. Playing golf at a resort isn't cheap.

But there was another reason why I wanted to play: George didn't look very athletic and I thought I might be able to beat him. Now, I'm not proud of myself for thinking that, but when you're not very good, like I was, then beating anyone—even when that person is paying your way—becomes a worthwhile goal.

But all hope of beating George vanished on the first hole. I teed off first, my drive slicing violently into the right rough. George then hit a beautiful fade that landed in the middle of the fairway, in perfect position for his next shot.

George marched briskly down the fairway and I veered off into the rough and began searching for my ball. Although a lifetime of poor play has made me very familiar with roughs, I often have trouble finding my ball there. I'd been looking for several minutes when George, standing next to his own ball, forty or fifty yards away, called back to me.

"Bob," he said, "Your ball is four yards in front of you and two yards to your left," as though he could actually see my ball from where he was standing, which I knew was impossible.

But not wanting to say anything to spoil our young friendship, I took four big steps forward and two big steps to my left. And there was my ball!

"I've got it, George, thanks," I called back, puzzled how he could have seen my ball from so far away. Just luck? Maybe.

My next shot was better than my drive, the ball settling a few yards to the left of the green. At least I was within striking distance. With a good chip I could still par the hole.

Meanwhile, George had punched a nice shot from the middle of the fairway onto the green, the ball rolling to within ten feet of the flag.

"Great shot, George," I called cheerfully, hiding my disappointment that he was playing so well. George acknowledged my compliment with a wave of his hand and we both walked toward the green.

George's ball was already on the green and mine wasn't, so it was still my turn to play. My next shot came out faster than I expected, the ball took a giant bounce on the far side of the green and landed in a sand trap. Unfortunately, it was still my turn.

On my next shot, I blasted the ball out of the trap onto the center of the green, but it was still farther from the pin than George's. I putted to within three feet of the hole and marked my ball. Then

George putted, just missing the cup. He tapped in and I holed my ball on the next putt. We walked off the green together, George with an easy par four and me with a tough double bogey six.

I won't bother to describe the remaining seventeen holes in any detail. It was clear that George, despite his unexceptional appearance, was a pretty exceptional golfer. He was playing great golf while I continued to struggle, but after a few holes I didn't mind. Although I usually dislike playing with golfers who are that much better than I am, George was a wonderful playing partner. He was never critical of my play nor of the many delays my poor shots caused us, and he was always supportive and helpful. When I managed to hit a decent shot he was quick to compliment me and explain what I had done right.

He also began suggesting ways I might improve my shots. Although I usually hate it when a playing partner does that, George did it in such a kind, helpful manner that I didn't mind, and as we continued our round my play got better and better. In fact, I actually parred the last three holes and that felt very good. As far as I could remember, I'd never parred three holes in a row before. Ever. Hooray for me.

George's suggestions, unlike those of the many golf professionals I'd paid to make me a better golfer, consisted of simple changes to my stance or swing that were easy to make. He told me to shorten my backswing, stand farther from the ball, and relax my hands, and when I did those things, my shots improved. When I hit a poor shot it was usually because I hadn't followed one or more of his suggestions. The discovery that my golf, though still far from good, was at least improvable made me think that maybe I wasn't as hopeless as I had previously thought, and in golf hope means a lot.

But as helpful as he was at improving my swing, his ability to find my lost balls bordered on the miraculous. Sometimes, when we were seventy-five or eighty yards apart and I was searching through tall grass and weeds, he would casually glance my way and tell me exactly where to find my ball. And he was never wrong.

When we finished playing, George asked if I wanted to go to the clubhouse for something to eat or drink and I said I did. Since George had so generously paid for my golf and had helped me improve my play—not to mention all the money and strokes he'd saved me by finding my lost balls—I felt that the very least I could do was pay for whatever he wanted. So, I ordered a club sandwich and an ice tea, but George only wanted bottled water.

But since buying a bottle of water isn't much of a thank you, I still felt a need to thank him for what had become a very wonderful afternoon. So before our order arrived I said, "George, I'm sorry that you just ordered water because I had really hoped to be able to repay you, at least a little for…"

"No, Bob," he answered, "The pleasure was all mine. It was so nice of you to play golf with a total stranger on such short notice."

"Yes, George," I said, persisting, "that's true, but at the same time it's been a great day for me. I've always had this crazy love-hate relationship with golf. That may be difficult for a good golfer like you to understand, but today you showed me some things and because of that I'll play better in the future. That's pretty great and…"

"It was nothing, Bob," he said, "any golfer would have done the same."

About that time I was becoming a little irritated by all his modesty, but I decided to try one more time. "George, besides showing me how to play better, you found my lost balls and you even paid my greens fee. You've been extremely generous and I just wanted to tell you how much I've appreciated it and how much I've enjoyed the afternoon. Thank you."

But George didn't respond and for the first time since I'd met him, his perfect little smile wasn't there. Then to my even greater surprise, George's eyes became moist and he looked positively miserable, emotions I had come to believe he wasn't capable of.

And that made me feel even worse. Had I been too hard on him? I thought not. On the contrary, all I'd done was compliment him and it seemed unlikely that praise would make someone sad.

I really had no explanation for what had just happened to George. Until a few minutes ago we'd been having what I thought was a very good time. So, trying to recapture that feeling I began asking about his family. What year in school was Charles? What sort of work did George do? Did they live here full-time or were they just vacationing? In response, George looked down at the table without answering and, if anything, appeared even more miserable. What in the world was going on? I didn't have a clue, so I just gave up.

The rest of our time together was very awkward. We walked to the car in silence and drove home without saying a word. He turned into the lot and parked. I pulled my clubs out of the trunk and hoisted them onto my shoulder.

Before going our separate ways I had planned to apologize for whatever it was that I must have said or done to change his mood so dramatically, but suddenly George turned to me, a tortured look on his face, and said, "Thanks for trying to cheer me up, Bob, but the fault isn't yours."

I was just about to ask if there was something I could do to help when George answered the question for me.

"Bob, we might need your help," he said, and without further explanation walked away toward his condominium.

11

Comparing Notes

I carried my clubs to our car and put them in the back, then walked to number sixty-four, opened the door, stepped over the fifty or so shoes sitting by the front door, and looked up to find the collective eyes of Caroline, Naomi, Clayton, Sam, and Mattie all pointed at me. I stared back, wondering what I had just walked into when Naomi came to my rescue.

"Bob, we're glad you're back," she said, "Caroline, Sam, and Clayton have gathered what I've been told is very important information about all the strange and confusing things that have been happening around here recently. I've heard some of it already, but not a lot. Professor Sam and his assistant, Miss Caroline, have been busy most of the day examining the new wildflowers and were unwilling to issue a statement until you got home. So, please have a seat and we can all hear what they've learned. It should be interesting."

I'd been so caught up in the events of my own day that I had nearly forgotten about our now-missing backyard visitor, and even worse, I had completely forgotten that when I left the house to play golf, Caroline and the kids were doing some investigating of their own.

"Could I get a beer first?" I asked.

Caroline pointed to the table next to an empty chair. "Your beverage awaits you, sire."

She knew me so well. I sat down.

Then Naomi said, "Sam, why don't you and Caroline give us your report first. Tell us what you've learned about the flowers."

Sam scrunched down in his seat. He glanced around the room, then picked up the topmost of several pages of notes resting in his lap, studied it, and began talking.

"Well," he said, "This morning Grandma Caroline took some of the new wildflowers out of the ground and examined them. Grandma Caroline likes to work in the garden so she knows a lot about flowers. She told me that even though the new flowers looked real, they didn't smell real and she wanted me to help her find out why."

He changed pages. "Well, we've been working on this all day and we've found three things wrong with the flowers. First, Grandma Caroline was right about the smell. When I smelled the flowers they didn't smell like real flowers and even the dirt around them didn't smell like real dirt. In fact, the flowers and the dirt didn't have any smell at all!"

He reached for the next page and continued. "Second, the roots of the wildflowers looked funny. None of the roots were longer than a certain length and the longer roots looked like they'd been chopped off. But Grandma Caroline said she hadn't cut them;

she'd just pulled them out of the ground. If the flowers were real, they shouldn't have looked like that."

"NOW," he said, glancing around the room, a mischievous grin on his face, "NUMBER THREE IS ABOUT SEX. This part is X-RATED. I'm going to tell you about MALE AND FEMALE REPRODUCTIVE ORGANS AND ABOUT HOW MOST FLOWERS ARE BISEXUAL, SO IF ANY OF YOU ARE UNCOMFORTABLE TALKING OPENLY ABOUT SEX THEN YOU SHOULD LEAVE THE ROOM RIGHT NOW."

Laughing, Naomi said, "Sam, I think everyone's comfortable talking about plant reproduction. So, go ahead and tell us what you've learned. And please, Sam, turn the volume down a little."

"OK," he said, reaching for another page, "Sorry. Well, real flowers have reproductive parts that are called stamens and pistils. Stamens are the male parts and they produce pollen. Pistils are the female parts and they produce ovules.

Most flowers are bisexual. That means that both the male and female parts are on the same plant. But that's not always the way they are. Sometimes flowers are just male or female, or they can start out one way and end up another. Sort of like us. But the important thing to remember is that ALL FLOWERS HAVE PARTS FOR REPRODUCTION BUT WHEN I LOOKED AT THE NEW WILDFLOWERS UNDER THE MICROSCOPE THEY DIDN'T HAVE ANY MALE OR FEMALE PARTS AT ALL!"

I thought Sam had finished, but instead he changed pages and kept going.

"Then Grandma Caroline had a good idea. She thought we should look at some of the real wildflowers and make sure they were different than the new wildflowers. So we took wildflowers from other parts of the backyard and looked at them under the microscope AND THEY WEREN'T THE SAME AS THE NEW WILDFLOWERS. ALL THE REAL WILDFLOWERS HAD BOTH SEXES AND THEIR ROOTS WEREN'T CHOPPED OFF."

Sam put his papers down and looked first at Caroline and then at his mom, a goofy grin on his face, "THEREFORE, THE NEW WILDFLOWERS ARE FAKE! WE REST OUR CASE."

Now that was impressive! Sam sounded like a real scientist and Caroline wasn't half-bad herself. I began applauding and everyone joined in. Sam got up and took several deep bows and Caroline waved her hand in a queenly manner.

"Thank you Caroline, thank you Sam," Naomi said, "That was very good. Are there any questions?"

"Caroline and Sam," I said, "That was great. Thank you. Your observations were smart and Sam, you were so clever to look at those flowers under your microscope. So here's my question: if the wildflowers aren't real then how were they made?"

Sam and Caroline looked at each other and Caroline answered. "I didn't know, but the professor here said that something called a three dimensional printer could've made the flowers. Maybe Sam would be kind enough to tell us about 3-D printers."

"NO! I WON'T TELL YOU ANY MORE OF MY SECRETS! YOU KNOW TOO MUCH ALREADY!" Sam said with a heavy accent, rolling his eyes like a mad scientist. Then grinning he said, "But maybe I will."

"Regular printers make images in two dimensions. Everything they produce is flat. But by laying down layers of plastic or metal on top of one another, a three-dimensional printer can take things that have depth, like a spoon or a toy or a part from a machine, and copy them. 3-D printers are pretty new but they're getting better all the time. But to make something as complicated as those fake wildflowers, a 3-D printer would have to be pretty advanced."

"So, Sam," I asked, "are you saying that an advanced 3-D printer could make copies of real wildflowers that seemed real at least until you looked at them under the microscope?"

"Well, maybe," he said, "but I didn't get the idea for the 3-D printer by looking at the fake flowers under the microscope. I got it when I saw that none of their roots were longer than a certain length and that all the bigger roots were chopped off and had flat ends. When I wondered how that might have happened that made me think of a 3-D printer."

I was confused. "Why would that make you think of a 3-D printer?"

"Let's say your 3-D printer isn't big enough to copy all the flowers completely—from their tops to the bottom of their roots—but you still wanted to make them look as real as you could. Then you might set the printer to copy everything above the ground—the part that people will see—but to copy just a part of what was below the ground. If you did that then all the roots that were longer than what your copier could copy would be chopped off, just like the roots of the phony flowers."

I was impressed. "Okay," I said, "that makes sense. Thanks."

"Sam," Caroline said, "When you first told me about 3-D printers you said you didn't think that the printers available now were good enough to copy something as complicated as that entire patch of wildflowers plus all the dirt."

"Yeah," he said, "even though the fake flowers aren't perfect they're still pretty amazing. I checked the Internet and the stuff that even the best 3-D printers can copy isn't nearly as complicated as those flowers, even with their missing parts."

"So, Sam," said Naomi, sounding confused, "what does that mean?"

"It means there really are 3-D printers that good. They're just not shown on the Internet."

"But why wouldn't they be on the Internet?" she asked.

"I don't know," he said, shrugging, "maybe they're experimental."

The room got very quiet.

Finally, Naomi said, "Thanks, Sam and Caroline, that was very interesting—maybe a little spooky—but very interesting. Are there any other questions for Sam and Caroline?"

Silence.

"No more questions," she said, "then it's Clayton's turn to tell us what he's learned today."

"Well, okay," said Clayton, looking at the floor and swinging his legs nervously back and forth, " but I don't think what I saw was nearly as good as what Sam and Grandma Caroline found out, but I'll tell you about it and you can decide for yourselves.

"My job today was to go around and find out what the other kids on the Ranch were talking about and the first place I went was the video game place where a lot of the kids hang out."

Mountainview's arcade was in a building near the swimming pool and tennis courts. It had a Ping-Pong table, a pool table, a pinball machine, and several coin-operated video games from the 1980s. Although the Ping-Pong was free, everything else cost something to play, usually twenty-five cents a game. Because Naomi preferred that her kids play outside she was not a big fan of the arcade.

Clayton looked nervously at Naomi, "And mom, I know you don't like us going there but I thought it would be a good place to hear things and I didn't play any of the games. I just listened."

"Clayton I appreciate your honesty," Naomi assured him, smiling, "but keep going. I want to know what happened next."

Looking relieved, Clayton continued. "Well, okay. So when I got to the arcade there were these two older guys playing some of the games and I heard them talking about this weird little kid who comes in every day and plays pinball and video games and he's so good that he's sort of amazing."

Then Clayton paused and looked around the room, once again swinging his legs.

"And the kid walks in."

"DUDE, FOR REAL? Sam exploded. HE JUST WALKED IN?"

"Yeah, he walks in and he sort of looks around but he doesn't say anything and he just starts playing, and, Dude, he was so good, I mean he played the games and beat them all and he could have played there all day just on free games, but he was there for about an hour and all at once he just stopped playing and walked out without saying anything to anybody."

"How fascinating!" said Naomi. "Did you learn any more about him?"

"Maybe a little. After he left I asked the guys what else they knew and they said he'd already been here a couple of months and that he must be pretty shy because he never talked to anyone and he didn't seem to have any friends, at least they'd never seen him with anyone, and every day he was there for about an hour and left, just like today."

"Interesting," said Naomi, "anything else?"

"Oh yeah, I almost forgot," Clayton answered, "They said that his family was staying in condo sixty-eight or sixty-nine and both of those are close to us but I've never seen him around."

Another pause and Naomi asked, "Anything else, Clayton?"

Clayton shook his head. "No," he said, "I went to some other places and asked around but that was the only good stuff I got."

"Thanks, Clayton," she said, "Nice work. Any questions?"

The room was quiet.

Then Naomi turned to me, smiling, "Well, Bob, we know you've been playing golf, but did you learn anything today?"

"Yes, I did," I said, surprised that she would ask. "When I left to play golf, I had no idea anything would come of it, but I was wrong. But before I tell you what happened I'd like to thank Clayton for telling us about the boy at the arcade because some of what I learned may have something to do with that same boy."

I was doing my best to remain calm but after hearing Clayton's report I could barely contain myself. His information about the boy—who I was betting was Charles Brown—fit beautifully with everything I'd learned about his father.

Then I told them about my strange and wonderful day with George Brown beginning with the odd way he had asked me to play golf, followed by meeting his wife, Linda, and their son, Charles, and their unusual love of snow cones. Next, I described how generous and kind George had been by paying for my golf, showing me ways to improve my game, and his astonishing ability to find my lost balls. And finally I told them that despite his ordinary appearance, George was an exceptional golfer. Then I stopped. I'd given them a lot of information and they'd need some time to digest it.

Clayton was the first to speak. "So, Grandpa Bob, what did George's son look like?"

"He was probably eight or nine, about Sam's age," I said, "but he was quite a bit shorter than Sam; maybe three or four inches shorter. His hair was dark brown, about the same color as yours, but cut short, and he was wearing a green University of Oregon T-shirt with a big yellow "O" right in the middle."

"That's him, Grandpa Bob!" Clayton said excitedly, "That's the kid from the arcade!"

"And, Clayton," I said, my excitement now rising to match his own, "you said the boys at the arcade told you his family was staying in condo sixty-eight or sixty-nine?"

Clayton nodded.

"Well, that fits, too. The Brown's condo is number sixty-eight!"

"Wow! That's so weird!" said Clayton, "And just think about the stuff they're both good at; George is really good at golf and Charles is really good at video games."

"And don't forget George's eyesight," Caroline said, "I've never heard of anyone being able to see that well."

"I thought the same thing," said Sam. "You can learn to be good at video games and golf but you can't learn to see like that."

The room got very quiet.

"So, what does it mean?" Clayton said softly to no one in particular.

"What do you think it means, Clayton?" his mom asked.

He looked at her thoughtfully and said, "Well, if you take what Grandma Caroline and Sam found out about the flowers and what Grandpa Bob and I found out about George and Charles, and you add in that weird thing in our back yard—and this may sound sort of crazy—but maybe the Browns are from somewhere else."

"Somewhere else?" Naomi asked. "Like what kind of somewhere else are you thinking of, Clayton?"

"Well…like…maybe…I don't know…like maybe they're from another planet," he said. "That kind of somewhere else. Like maybe they're aliens."

Sam jumped up, a big smile on his face, his blue eyes dancing. "BUT DUDE, IF THE BROWNS WERE ALIENS THEY'D HAVE FOURTEEN EYES, AND BE WEARING SPACE

SUITS, AND HAVE LASER GUNS SO THEY COULD VAPORIZE US!"

But as though he hadn't heard his brother, Clayton continued, "The weird thing is that if the Browns are really aliens they don't seem very scary. I mean if we'd never met the Browns before and someone said, 'Oh, yeah, did you know that the family staying in number 68 is from another planet,' we'd be scared, right? But right now we're just talking about them like, 'Oh, yeah, the Browns, they're this nice family from outer space so maybe some night we should have them over for hamburgers."

"NO, CLAYTON! NOT HAMBURGERS!" roared Sam, "THEY ONLY EAT SNOW CONES!"

"Right," I said, laughing. "So Sam, how do you think the Browns might fit with that thing that landed in our back yard?"

I thought this might slow him down, but it didn't. Without missing a beat Sam was ready with an answer. "Well, maybe it's important to them in some way we don't understand. Like there was that big thing, right, and inside the big thing there were all these smaller things, and maybe inside each of those is some kind of special food or chemical that they need to stay alive."

It sounded reasonable.

"OK," I said. "But if the thing in the backyard is connected to the Browns, then how do the fake wildflowers fit in?"

Naomi spoke up. "While Sam was explaining the 3-D printer I had this idea about how everything might fit together. To start with, if that thing in the back yard is connected to the Browns—and it probably is—then the fake wildflowers were made by the Browns to cover the spot where the thing landed, but because the flowers are too complicated to have been made by one of our 3-D printers they were made by a more advanced printer that the Browns brought with them from their own planet!"

Naomi took a deep breath and shivered. "It's sort of creepy!"

"Well, it doesn't sound that great to me either, but it makes sense," said Caroline. "So, should we call Officer Sally and have her check them out?"

But that made me uncomfortable. It sounded like the Browns were having problems of their own, and if so, the last thing they needed right now was a police investigation.

"I wouldn't do that," I said. "The Browns haven't broken any laws and they seem like nice people, and nothing that I've seen makes me think they're dangerous. In fact, they seem just the opposite; like they're going out of their way to be good citizens."

"You know," said Clayton, "aliens in movies are usually bad, but they don't have to be that way; there could be good aliens, too. Like maybe some are good and some are bad."

"I'm no expert on aliens," I said, "but no matter where people are from they have families and jobs, so it stands to reason that most aliens would be peaceful and friendly, at least to each other."

Then I paused. "But now," I said, "I need to tell you something else that happened today because it may help us decide what to do about the Browns."

"What's that?" asked Clayton, his eyes wide.

"When George and I had finished our golf we went to the clubhouse for something to eat and because of George's generosity it had been a very good day for me and I wanted to let him know how much I appreciated it. So, I began thanking him for all the nice things he'd done, but the more I talked the sadder he looked, which seemed very strange. So, I tried to cheer him up but it didn't work, and after that we hardly spoke to each other. We drove home and were just about to go our separate ways when suddenly he thanked me for trying to cheer him up and said, 'Bob, we might need your help.'"

"Wow!" exclaimed Clayton, "He said they might need your help! That's so weird! What do you think he meant?"

"I'm not sure," I said, "after that he just walked away."

"So, Bob," said Caroline solemnly, "after hearing him say that, what are you going to do?"

An alarm went off in my head. Sometimes, when Caroline asked me a question like 'So, Bob, what are you going to do?' it really meant that she knew exactly what I was supposed to do and if I didn't then I would likely find myself with a very unhappy wife. If that was what her question meant, and I was pretty sure it did, experience had taught me that the best thing to do was to find out what she wanted me to do and do it.

"I'm not sure," I lied, "You're much better with the psychological stuff than I am. What do you think I should do?"

"Well, I agree with you now about not calling the police," she said, "but I think you need to talk to George and find out why he was so upset. Whatever was on his mind was obviously very upsetting. So, if I were you I'd find out what that is and I'd do it sooner rather than later."

"You mean like tonight?" I asked without much enthusiasm.

"Yes."

I stared back at her without speaking. With no idea what we might be getting ourselves into, I was considerably less certain about talking to George than she was. As much as I liked him, the thought of becoming involved in his family's problems made me uneasy. But Caroline was looking at me like talking to George tonight was exactly what she expected me to do.

"OK," I said reluctantly, "After dinner I'll ask George if he wants to talk and if he says 'yes,' then where should we go?"

"What about the Alpine Lounge at the lodge?" she said. "That seems like a perfect place to talk. The booths are private and it should be quiet tonight."

"But," I asked innocently, "aren't you worried that he might vaporize me while we're there?"

"NO!" Sam declared; "HE WON'T VAPORIZE YOU IF OTHER PEOPLE ARE AROUND. HE'LL WAIT UNTIL YOU LEAVE THE LODGE. THE LAWN NEXT TO THE TENNIS COURTS WOULD BE PERFECT!"

"Oh, really," I said, smiling uneasily, "it sounds like you've given this a lot of thought, Sam, like maybe you and George have already talked about it."

"It's possible," he said mysteriously, "but so are a lot of things."

"Bob and Sam!" snapped Naomi, "I think we've heard enough about being vaporized. Would you give it a rest, please?"

There was no further mention of vaporization and after dinner I went upstairs and showered, changed into my nicest clothes and walked up the boardwalk to condo number sixty-eight, hoping that I looked a lot more confident than I felt.

12

The Alpine Lounge

I knocked several times before Linda finally opened the door, but instead of greeting me she looked nervously around as though checking to see if I was alone. Satisfied that I was, she motioned me into the house but immediately locked the door.

Though still smiling, she looked frazzled and much less pleased to see me than she had earlier today. She called upstairs and when George came down he, too, looked rattled.

What in the world was going on? Could I have misinterpreted his parting words to mean something that they didn't or was their odd behavior a sign of something else?

George and I sat down across from each other at the dining room table and Linda hurriedly asked if I wanted something to eat or drink. When I thanked her and said no she nodded and ran up stairs.

Since I was no longer certain that what I was about to say would be welcome, I decided to deliver my message as quickly as possible and get out of there before I got vaporized.

"George," I said, "the last thing you told me this afternoon was that your family might need my help. I'm curious to know how I might be able help you. If you'd like to talk about it, I'm available. If so, we could stay here or, if you'd like, we could go to the Alpine Lounge at the lodge and talk there. The Lounge should be quiet tonight and the booths there are very private, but it's up to you."

As though hearing welcome news, George visibly relaxed.

"Bob," he said, a relieved smile on his face, "I told Linda this afternoon that I had said something to you about needing your help, but we had no idea how you would react. I thought that my strange behavior might have frightened you and Linda was convinced you would call the police. I'm happy we were wrong. Yes, I would love to talk, and yes, the lodge sounds perfect."

"George," I said, "I'm so relieved to hear you say that. I was afraid I'd misunderstood you."

"No," said George, "You understood me perfectly. Give me a minute to tell Linda and I'll be right back."

George ran upstairs and returned promptly, a smile on his face. We left the condo and walked down the boardwalk, past the arcade, across a broad, well-tended expanse of grass, around the pool and tennis courts to the lodge. If I was really walking next to someone from another planet, it felt strangely comfortable. But as we crossed the lawn I couldn't help thinking about Sam's statement that here would be the perfect spot for George to vaporize me. Though the memory made me smile, it also reminded me how little I really knew about George. I would need to be cautious.

We walked up the steps to the lodge, I held the big wood and glass door open, and we went inside. It was Sunday night, well past dinnertime, and just as Caroline had predicted, the lodge was very quiet. A few diners were finishing up in the restaurant below us. We climbed the winding wooden staircase to the Alpine Lounge and there a smiling young woman led us to a booth where the only light was a candle flickering faintly behind dark glass. I ordered a Coke and as expected, George ordered bottled water.

The waitress left and George and I sat looking at each other across the dimly lit table. George cleared his throat and began speaking.

"First of all, Bob, thank you for suggesting that we talk tonight. I have been reluctant to discuss this with anyone but it must be done. The truth is that my family and I are in a very difficult situation."

"So you really might need my help?"

"Yes," he said, "it's very possible. But the reason why requires some explanation, so I hope you're not in a hurry."

I shook my head. "Don't worry, I've got plenty of time."

"Then I'll begin at the beginning," he said. "First of all, I should confess that when I asked you to play golf this morning, the real reason was somewhat different than what I told you at the time. I did it more to gain an introduction to you and your family than I did to play golf, although I enjoy playing golf, too."

"That doesn't surprise me," I said. "And as I'm sure you know something very strange happened at our house last night. While the boys were outside looking for golf balls they discovered an unusual object that later disappeared."

"Yes," said George, "I know that, too, just as you know that I was the person standing at the window, watching you and your daughter-in-law examine our biological container."

"Your...biological container?" I asked.

"Yes. That's what we call it," he said, "because it's made of living tissue."

"Interesting," I said as matter-of-factly as I could, even though I found the idea of a living container a little unsettling.

"And since the container landed," George continued, "you and your family have been working very hard to unravel the mystery of its arrival and disappearance. We knew it was only a matter of time before you connected us to the container.

"But long before you began investigating the container we've been watching your family. In fact, we've been studying the Davises since they arrived a month ago and we've been interested in you and your wife since you arrived last Friday."

His admission that they'd been "studying" the Davises and "interested" in Caroline and me made me uneasy. I knew it was time to ask him the big question.

"George," I said, "before we go any further I need to ask you something. I'd like to..."

But just then the waitress arrived with our drinks. Smiling, she placed them on coasters and asked if we'd like anything else. We told her no, she thanked us and left.

I began again. "George," I said, "I need to ask you a very important question, but before I do I'd like to tell you something about myself."

I paused, collecting my thoughts. "By nature," I said, "I'm a trusting person. It's just the way I am. But sometimes I'm too trusting and end up getting hurt. I'm sure you can understand how that might happen."

George nodded. "Yes, of course I do."

I continued. "Although I've known you for less than twelve hours, in that short time I've come to believe that you're a kind, honest person who would never hurt other people. So, George, my question is: 'Are you the person I think you are, or by trusting you am I putting my family in danger?'"

George sat quietly for a moment before speaking. "Bob," he said solemnly, "Although I could tell you that your family is in absolutely no danger and leave it at that, I would rather have you listen to my story and decide for yourself if I'm worthy of your trust."

"Okay," I said, "that's seems fair."

And George began his story.

"By now you probably know that we are not native to your planet and if you didn't then I'm sure you at least suspected it."

Although that was exactly what I expected him to say, it was still a shock to hear him say it.

"You're right," I said as evenly as I could, "we thought that might be the case."

George nodded and continued.

"Our planet exists in a solar system very similar to yours but with one big difference: our planet revolves around the sun in an orbit that overlaps the orbit of another planet with which we share a moon. The orbits of the two planets cross each other twice a year. The moon that we share follows our planet for half the year and then, when the other planet passes closer to the moon than does our own, it's gravitational field pulls the moon away from us and holds it for the rest of the year, until once again our planet takes it back. I'm sure that sounds like a very strange arrangement to you, but because that's the way it's always been, to us it feels normal."

George poured himself some water, took a long drink, and continued. "Both planets are populated by the same race of people. Although humanity originated on our planet, once space travel became possible it was easy to colonize the other planet.

"These two planets are named the Twins and because human life began on our planet it is called Twin One, or just One, while the other planet is Twin Two, or just Two.

"For the past hundred years the moon that we share has been the source of something that keeps the people of both planets alive. If I told you the name of that substance in our language it would sound very strange, but when it is translated into your language it becomes 'water of life,' which in your ancient Latin language is 'aqua vitae (ak-wah VEE-tay).'" Because 'aqua vitae' is easier to say we prefer using it to 'water of life.' The biological container that landed in your backyard two nights ago was filled with packets of aqua vitae.

"Throughout the early history of our planet, aqua vitae was present in great abundance but because of population growth and wasteful practices it decreased until around two hundred years ago our people faced extinction.

"But then two fortunate events occurred: space travel became possible and because of that, huge deposits of aqua vitae were discovered on Twin Two. Suddenly we had the means of going to and from Twin Two and what seemed like an unlimited supply of aqua vitae. More importantly, the settlers of Twin Two saw their aqua vitae as belonging to everyone, and shared it freely with the people of both planets. Once again the future looked bright.

"But as time passed problems again arose. For the same reasons as before, the aqua vitae on Twin Two dwindled until once again we faced another crisis. Then aqua vitae was discovered on the moon.

"But this brought with it a new set of problems. Once aqua vitae was found on the moon the relationship between the two planets changed. Knowing that the moon's supply might be our last, the people of both planets became selfish. Control of the moon and its aqua vitae now shifted back and forth depending on the moon's position. For the six months that the moon was ours we had plenty of aqua vitae, but for the next six months, when the moon belonged to Twin Two, we relied on our reserves. For both planets it was feast-or-famine, but at least it was predictable and in its own way fair.But at the same time we knew that there would come a time when even that system would fail.

"And in fact, that time has come. Recently we learned that Twin Two's military now controls the moon and is threatening war if we attempt to take more aqua vitae. A peaceful solution is being sought, but so far without success.

"To make matters worse, the moon is running out of aqua vitae. Scientists estimate that its deposits will last only a few more years.

"Five years ago, knowing that these problems were inevitable, our government sent people to other planets in search of aqua vitae. Likely planets were identified and appropriate families selected, and as part of that program we were sent to Earth.

"But the results of this project have been disappointing. None of the families have found aqua vitae. Of course, further investigation could change that, but not in time to help us now. Unless an immediate solution to our problems is found, the supply of aqua vitae that we received two nights ago will be our last and we will be forced to return home. And for us, the prospect of returning home empty-handed after all our sacrifice is heartbreaking and the fact that we love it here in Oregon makes our sadness even worse."

Then George's face became red and splotchy and he held a napkin to his eyes. He took another drink of water and asked if he might take a brief break to collect himself. I said that would be fine, he thanked me then stood and disappeared down the stairs.

I felt terrible for George. His comment that he and his family were in "a very difficult situation" was certainly the understatement of the year. What was happening to the Twins was a tragedy of the first order.

But the longer I sat there waiting for him to return, the more I began to question the reality of what I had just heard. Aliens? Spaceships? Two planets warring over something called aqua vitae? Could this be real?

Yes, I told myself, as strange as it all sounded it had to be real. Didn't it? But what if it wasn't? What if everything I had just seen and heard was no more than an elaborate dream? I tried to think of some way to confirm its reality and saw George's glass and water bottle sitting across from me.

I reached out and touched them. Yes, they were there all right, but what did that mean? Probably not much, and looking across at George's place at the table I saw no other evidence that he'd ever been there.

But if this was a dream it was by far the best dream I'd ever had and I didn't want it to end. So, hoping to keep whatever this was—dream or reality, at that moment I didn't care—from disappearing, I sat very still.

But after a couple of minutes of this I felt foolish. What was I doing? The answer was obvious; I was trying to avoid the truth. Was that what I wanted to do? No, it wasn't. I needed to know the truth, and if the truth was that I was dreaming then I would wake myself up.

So, with that in mind I began wiggling around in my seat. But after a few minutes of wiggling nothing had changed; I was still in the Alpine Lounge waiting for George to return from downstairs. So I wiggled even harder. Still nothing. Then, in addition to wiggling I began swinging my arms from side to side.

"Sir," said a voice beside me, "are you all right?"

It was the waitress. I halted my gyrations and felt myself blush, hoping the room was too dark for her to see.

"No, I'm fine," I said, trying to sound reassuring, "but thanks for your concern. No, I was just loosening up some sore muscles. I'm afraid I'm not used to all the exercise I've been getting. But as long as you're here would you mind getting us another round of drinks?"

"No, of course not," she said, "and I'm glad it was just sore muscles. I thought you were having a seizure."

The waitress disappeared and returned promptly with our drinks just as George was coming up from downstairs.

He looked much better, and now knowing that I was neither dreaming nor crazy, I probably did, too.

"So, Bob," he said, smiling, "after all the strange things I've just told you, you probably have some questions. So please, ask me anything."

"You're right, George," I said, smiling back at him, "that was a pretty wild story and I do have a few questions. My first is 'what's so special about aqua vitae?'"

"Aqua vitae is a mixture of several different chemicals," he said, "but the ingredient that keeps us alive is a complex, carbon-based molecule built around an unusual metal and despite all our knowledge and technical ability we have never been able to make it for ourselves."

"Your planet seems so advanced," I said, "I'm amazed you can't make anything you want. But thanks for telling me. My next question is 'when will you find out if you're staying or leaving?'"

"In the next day or two."

"Really!" I said, surprised that it would be so soon. "And if you have to leave when would that be?"

"As soon as possible."

"Wow!" I said, shocked. "I thought you might be able to stay awhile. The aqua vitae that we saw the other night looked like quite a lot.

"Unfortunately," he said, "it's not as much as it looks. Each container holds about two hundred packets. Each packet is a day's worth of aqua vitae for one person, so a large container like that will last three people a little more than two months. If we leave we would need to add whatever is left to the aqua vitae already on board the spaceship."

"Well, I'm sorry to hear that," I said. "I was hoping to spend some more time with you. But I guess there's still a chance you might stay. My last question is: 'why did you pick me to help you?'"

"We've always known that at some point in our travels we could find ourselves facing a shortage of aqua vitae, so no matter where we were we had to plan for that possibility. It was like a game we always played. But living on Earth has created an unusual set of circumstances, and as much as we'd like to handle all the arrangements ourselves, we simply can't. Knowing that we might need help, we've been watching the people here at Mountainview, looking for a family we could use if we had to go home."

Uh-oh. I didn't like that.

"George, first of all you said "a family" rather than just "a person." Would helping you involve our whole family, rather than just me?"

"Yes," he answered, "I'm afraid it would."

I liked that even less.

"And then you said you were looking for a family you could use. I guess it's the word "use" that bothers me. How would you be using us? It sounds threatening."

George smiled. "Yes, you're right," he said, "What I said could be interpreted to mean we might have to do something unpleasant to you, but, of course, that's not what I meant. I should have said we thought we could turn to you and your family for help. I didn't mean that we would need to kidnap your family and take them with us to our planet."

"Well, that's reassuring," I said, returning his smile, "but I'm afraid I was thinking of something else. Something very different."

"Oh," said George, "what was that?"

"Promise me you won't be offended."

"I promise."

"I thought that you might have to eat us."

"Eat you?" he said, pausing to consider this. "Why would you think that?"

"Because our bodies could contain the special ingredient in aqua vitae."

"Well yes, that's true," he answered seriously. "But of course we wouldn't need to eat all of you. A few arms and legs, a head or two, certainly no more than that."

What! He wasn't serious, was he? I searched his face for a sign that he was joking and when he finally broke into a guilty smile we both erupted into loud, raucous laughter. Our outburst was completely out of place in the quiet, intimate atmosphere of the Alpine

Lounge, but I didn't care. It had been a long and very tense day and it felt wonderful to laugh.

Midway through our hysterics the waitress arrived to check on us. Tears, seizures, and now uncontrollable laughter; we must have been the craziest customers she'd ever had. We assured her that we'd never felt better.

Still laughing, George said, "Since we've been here, one of our greatest pleasures has been watching the science fiction channel on TV. We've gotten enormous pleasure from seeing how Hollywood portrays us. We're usually hideous, completely unlikeable, and constantly inventing new ways to mistreat you."

"Yes, that's true," I said, "but at least you dress well."

It was almost eleven when we finally left the lounge. As George and I crossed the grassy area I told him that it was here that my grandson, Sam, thought that George might try to vaporize me.

"Really? Vaporize you? That boy has a good head on his shoulders doesn't he? Yes, it would have been an excellent spot, but dumb me I left my ray gun at home. Please tell him I'm sorry and that I'll get you next time."

72

13

Home Again

Though it was late, everyone except Mattie was up waiting for me when I arrived, still smiling, back at our condo.

"Judging from the size of that grin," Caroline said, "I gather things went well between you boys."

"Yes, they did," I said. "We had a wonderful conversation and it was good that we talked when we did. Thanks for suggesting it."

"So, Bob," Naomi asked, "are they really from another planet or did we just imagine that?"

"No, it was like we thought," I said so matter-of-factly I surprised myself, "George and his family are from another planet. They're here because of trouble back home."

"Oh, so that's it?" said Naomi, smiling, "More trouble back home. That's always their excuse, isn't it? You'd think that just once they could come up with something different."

"Naomi," I said, "I couldn't agree with you more. It shows a real lack of imagination on their part."

"Grandpa Bob!" Clayton scolded me, "Tell us what he said!!"

"Sorry, Clayton," I answered. "Well, it was just like Sam thought; their lives depend on the stuff in those little bags. George said that the name for it in English is "water of life," but in Latin it's 'aqua vitae,' and that's what they like to call it."

I took a deep breath and continued.

"Aqua vitae comes from a moon that goes back and forth between their planet and a neighboring planet. The two planets are called the Twins, Twin One and Twin Two. George and his family are from Twin One. He said that the Twins are running out of aqua vita and recently Twin Two's military invaded the moon and now controls all that's left.

"A few years ago, knowing that one day something like this would happen, Twin One's government sent several families to other planets looking for aqua vitae. The Browns are one of those families. Unfortunately, none of the families have discovered any aqua vitae, so unless the Twins find a quick solution to their problems, the Browns will need to go home."

I looked around the room. Everyone seemed to be accepting my explanation, but just as had happened at the Alpine Lounge I thought it sounded absurd. I stopped talking and shook my head in disbelief.

"I know what I'm saying sounds crazy," I said, "but when George was telling it to me it seemed perfectly reasonable."

"Don't worry, Grandpa Bob," said Clayton, "It sounds a little crazy but we still believe you. Keep going."

The others nodded their agreement.

Reassured, I continued. "And if they have to go home they'll need some help, so they've been studying the people at Mountainview, and of all the families here they like ours the best."

"Well, I guess that's a compliment," said Naomi, "but good grief, Bob, what kind of help are they going to need?"

"I'm not sure," I said, "but George said that there wouldn't be that much for us to do and there would be no risk. But he'd like to explain it to us in person so we can decide for ourselves."

Then I paused, uncertain if now was the best time to tell them something else that George and I had talked about, but it seemed as good a time as any.

"And Naomi," I said, "I probably should have discussed this with you first, but I invited them here for dinner tomorrow."

A long silence followed my announcement. Then Sam said, "DUDE, THAT'S SO COOL. WE'LL BE HAVING DINNER WITH SPACE PEOPLE."

"Dude," said Clayton, "when we get home our friends will ask about our summer and we'll say, 'well, it was just your average summer, not much happened but we did have a nice dinner with some people from outer space and we all ate snow cones.'"

Howling with laughter, Clayton rolled over and buried his head in the cushion of his chair while Sam fell helplessly onto the floor.

Then Naomi said, "It's okay, Bob. Dinner's not a problem. I've got an old family recipe for Samoan snow cones that I'm sure they'll love."

When I had recovered long enough for my brain to start working again, it occurred to me that even if the Browns whipped out their ray guns after dinner and vaporized us, it might still be worth it. Having dinner with a family from another planet could be something that no one else on Earth had ever done before.

Then I began imagining how dinner with the Browns might compare with the most important events the world has ever known. Would it be like Columbus discovering America, Lewis and Clarke reaching the Pacific Ocean, or Neil Armstrong walking on the moon? Maybe.

Then I imagined a picture of the historic dinner on a stamp or a souvenir dinner plate; a drawing of the two families sitting stiffly around the dinner table eating snow cones.

But tearing me from my fantasies like a bucket of ice water was the telephone. It was nearly midnight, who would be calling now?

Naomi muttered something under her breath and grabbed the phone. "Yes!" she snapped, then blushing with embarrassment said, "Oh, Sally, forgive me for being rude, but I had no idea it was you. No, we're still up. What were we doing? Well, we were…we were…"

Naomi put her hand over the phone and looked frantically around the room for help. Sam jabbed his finger at the TV, and nodding thankfully Naomi answered, "We were watching TV. That's right. What were we watching? Well, it's a movie…I'm not sure what its name is…but it's very good. What's it about? It's about aliens invading earth. Yes, I know, quite a coincidence isn't it? But now we're hooked and have to see how it ends. Anyway, it's good to hear from you, Sally. So, what have you learned?"

The seconds ticked by as Naomi listened.

"Yes..........yes.........yes..........no...no, Sally, that would be fine. You say he'll be here around ten? No, I'm sure we'll be up by then. No, the movie's almost over. Thanks for calling and thanks for all your help. Good night, Sally."

Naomi hung up.

"As I'm sure you heard," she said, "that was Officer Sally. She apologized for calling so late, but she wanted to let us know what had happened since she was here this morning and to give us a heads-up for tomorrow. Today at their noon meeting she told the other officers what we saw but none of them had seen or heard of anything like that before. She said that a couple of the guys thought we were probably just imagining the whole thing but when she told them that her investigation had confirmed our story, the guys shut up. Then someone said that the smaller bags could be drugs from some kind of Mexican smuggling operation, but when she told him that was ridiculous the other cops agreed with her.

"Then one of the guys suggested that she call the FBI office in Portland to see what they thought, and Sally's boss agreed. So this afternoon she called the FBI and the upshot is that a special agent will be coming out to talk to us tomorrow. She apologized for the inconvenience, but hoped we'd talk to him. I told her we would and she said he'd be here at ten o'clock tomorrow morning. She didn't know what agency he was with, just that he was some kind of hot-shot specialist who dealt with cases like ours."

That wasn't good news. A visit from a government agent could create big problems, both for us and for the Browns.

"I know she's trying to help," I said, "but if we tell him that the Browns are from another planet, even if he thinks we're crazy he'll want to talk to them and whatever happens after that could interfere with their trip home. But if we lie to him that might land us in trouble."

Then Naomi gave me her most penetrating, no-nonsense stare, and said, "Bob, just how sure are you that the Browns aren't a bunch of nuts, and if they're not nuts then how much do you really believe they're from another planet?"

Her questions went right to the heart of the matter. Except for Clayton seeing Charles at the arcade, I was the only one who knew anything about the Browns and though we were sure to learn more about them at tomorrow night's dinner, that would be well after the agent's visit.

I knew how important it was to answer Naomi's questions as accurately as I could. Wrong conclusions wouldn't help anyone. And though my initial impulse was to tell her that the Browns weren't nuts and that they were definitely from another planet, I knew that wasn't good enough. I had to weigh all the evidence both for and against the Browns being aliens before giving her my answer.

So, I put everything that I knew about the Browns into one of three categories. The categories were: strong evidence for them being aliens, weak evidence for them being aliens, and evidence against them being aliens.

In the strong-evidence-for category I put George's extraordinary eyesight and the strange biological container that had landed in our backyard. Those two seemed rock-solid.

In the "weak-evidence-for" category I put George's exceptional ability to play golf and his son's equally exceptional ability to play arcade games.

Then there were the snow cones. They were definitely strange, but if a family drank only bottled water and ate nothing but snow cones did that mean they were from another planet? Yes, I thought it did. At the very least, the snow cones belonged in the "weak-evidence-for" category. They were just too weird to ignore.

Then there was the extraordinary ordinariness of George and Linda's appearance and their perfect speech. Although those were odd, they didn't seem odd enough to belong in either of the "for" categories.

And finally, what evidence did I have that the Browns weren't aliens? Not much. Yes, they looked like us, talked like us, and acted like us, but that was about it.

Although there was still some chance I was wrong, the evidence for the Browns being aliens seemed pretty convincing.

"Naomi," I said, "I don't think the Browns are nuts and yes, I think they're from another planet. Sorry."

"OK," Naomi answered. "Then we'll need to discuss our strategy for tomorrow."

Two hours later we got to bed.

14

The Man From BETA

A few short hours after that we were up again, sitting at the dining room table having breakfast and reviewing our strategy before the special agent arrived. Our plan was simple enough that I thought it might work. We would describe the discovery and physical appearance of the container and our visit from Sally Justice, and that was it. Otherwise we didn't know a thing. We had no idea why the container disappeared, Caroline and Sam knew nothing about the wildflowers, and we'd never heard of the Browns.

At nine-thirty there was a knock at the front door and when I went to answer it I found myself face-to-face with two very large, serious-looking men, one black and one white. Except for their color differences they could have been twins. Both had military-style buzz cuts and wore sunglasses, white shirts, thin black ties, and black suits stretched tightly over their heavily muscled bodies. Both held out gold badges in leather holders and indicated that I should open the door. I obliged and both men pushed past me and began searching the house.

They checked the first floor rooms then went upstairs where we could hear them moving from floor to floor and room to room. When they returned to the ground floor, the white agent whispered something into his hand and the black agent announced, "Mr. Bond will be here shortly. The United States of America thanks you for your cooperation."

Then the black agent put a beefy hand over one ear, listening intently. Whatever he heard made him move quickly to the front hall just as the white agent moved to the sliding doors in back. Then, simultaneously, both men assumed the military rest position: legs spread, eyes straight ahead, hands joined in back.

Nothing happened for a few minutes and then there was a soft knock at the front door. Caroline went to answer it and I heard her say, "Hi, I'm Caroline, you must be Mr. Bond. Please come in, everyone's inside." I didn't hear a response, but then a small, stooped, and very elderly man pushing a walker shuffled slowly into the room.

Mr. Bond had thick, unruly white hair and eyebrows so dense they resembled two fat, white caterpillars. The thick lenses of his rimless eyeglasses magnified his milky blue eyes. Like the other men, he, too, wore a white shirt, a thin black tie, and a black suit, but unlike them Mr. Bond's suit was at least two sizes too big for him. He shambled unsteadily toward a dining room chair and collapsed into it. Removing a handkerchief from his coat, he looked deliberately about the room, his eyes settling briefly on each person before moving to the next. He put the handkerchief to his mouth, coughed a long, wet cough, cleared his throat, wiped his mouth, and arching his eyebrows expectantly, looked directly into my eyes.

"Tell me," he said with surprising forcefulness, "Everything."

Not sure why he had chosen me but afraid of displeasing him, I began talking. I described how the boys' golf ball business had led to their discovery of our backyard visitor, told him about my solo trip to the bag as well as Naomi's and my visit early yesterday morning. Then I described the bag's appearance, recounted Officer Justice's visit, mentioned the wildflowers, and stopped.

Silence.

Mr. Bond continued staring at me, his magnified blue eyes locked on mine. The room felt uncomfortably warm.

Finally he said, "Show me the flowers."

Our trip to the wildflowers took a while. With great effort Mr. Bond struggled into a standing position and with his agents beside him he moved gradually out of the house, over the deck, down the stairs, and across the lawn to where the wildflowers were. He stared at the flowers for a long time then raised his right hand and his agents lowered him into a kneeling position. He steadied himself on his walker, slipped his other hand into a coat pocket and pulled out a huge magnifying glass. After panning the glass deliberately across the flowers he returned it to his pocket.

Once more raising his hand, the agents helped him to his feet. Mr. Bond then straightened, turned, and moved slowly back toward the house. Inside, he caught his breath and sat down, his eyes searching the room until, once again, they found mine.

"Have they made contact?" he said.

It was show time. I shook my head and put a puzzled look on my face. "I'm sorry," I said with as much sincerity as I could muster, "who would have contacted us?" And as I waited for his answer I felt a large bead of sweat take a slow and very obvious trip down my forehead and into my right eye.

Mr. Bond's unblinking stare continued as the two white caterpillars crawled up his forehead into an angry scowl. Long seconds ticked by. Still frowning, he raised his right hand and the two agents moved to his side and helped him to his feet, and pushing his walker, he tottered across the floor in the direction of the front door. As he passed by, he pointed a gnarled finger at me and motioned me to follow. Then the four of us—Mr. Bond, his agents, and myself—moved haltingly forward until we reached the door. Once there, the white agent held it open as Mr. Bond, still scowling, again fixed his eyes on mine.

"The question is…what do they want? If it is something… that will put us in conflict…then you must let me know. If not…………....well………….savor the experience."

The caterpillars flattened, a faint smile flitted across his lips, and I felt him put something into my hand. Then, with his agents beside him, Mr. Bond shuffled slowly out the door and across the wooden walkway to the lot beyond. I watched until they were out of sight.

The screen door closed with a soft thump and I stood there, struggling to understand what I'd just been told. As Mr. Bond's parting words began to make sense, I started to panic. Did he really mean that everything—perhaps even the fate of the world—was riding on what we learned about the Browns tonight at dinner?

It seemed like an unreasonable responsibility to place on a family who had simply gathered three nights ago for a summer vacation. I ran through his words a few more times but always arrived at the same conclusion.

But then I remembered that what the Browns had come here for was aqua vitae and that George had already told me they hadn't found any. Did that mean we were safe?

Relaxing a little, I was suddenly conscious of whatever it was he had placed in my hand and glanced down to see. It was a business card that read:

Albert S. Bond

Chief Investigator

Department of Defense

Bureau of Extra-Terrestrial Affairs

5000 Defense Pentagon

Washington, DC 20301-5000

1 (703) 697-5131

The card's last line offered a tiny bit of reassurance. At least now, when the Browns whipped out their ray guns and opened fire, we had a number to call. I put the card in my wallet next to Officer Sally's.

When I returned to the living room once again all eyes were on me. Caroline spoke first. "Well, Bob, what did you and old Mr.

Bond talk about? Since it probably wasn't the weather, it would be nice if you would share it with the rest of us." That Caroline was one smart cookie.

"Well," I said, "as you just saw, Mr. Bond is a man of few words. At the door he told me that the question is what do they want. If it's something that will put us in conflict with them then we should let him know. But if not, then we should savor the experience.'"

"Mom," Clayton said, "What does the word 'savor' mean?"

"Clayton, the word 'savor' means that you should enjoy something as much as you can. Like if you're eating something really good then you should eat it slowly so you can enjoy it as long as possible."

"MOM," said Sam, "IT MEANS THAT IF YOU MEET UP WITH A BUNCH OF ALIENS AND THEY DON'T WANT TO VAPORIZE YOU THEN YOU SHOULD ENJOY BEING WITH THEM."

"Like if they're nice," Mattie added quietly.

Although it was reassuring that the kids' interpretation of Mr. Bond's message was exactly the same as mine, it was humbling to think that it had taken them less than half as long to reach the same conclusion. After this, if I had a question that needed a quick and accurate answer, rather than struggle with it myself I'd just ask someone between the ages of two and nine.

"So if he said that," Caroline said, "then he must have known you'd already made contact with the Browns. In other words, he saw right through your act."

She was right. When Mr. Bond first sat down and studied everyone, he wasn't looking for the family spokesperson or the smartest person in the room. He was looking for the person whose answers, even if they were intentionally misleading, would be the easiest to read. And that had been me.

"Caroline," I said a bit defensively, "You're right, but isn't it better that he knows the truth?"

"Then I guess it's good he didn't believe you," she said smugly.

Yes, she was right, but so what? Mr. Bond knew that I was lying and he was still okay with it.

I stood there for a while, marveling at just how clever the old guy had been. His body wasn't much, but there was nothing wrong with his brain.

Then I remembered something else that had happened at the front door. "In fact," I said, "right after he told me that he did something pretty amazing."

"What was that?" asked Clayton.

"He smiled," I said. "Not a giant smile, but a definite smile. Like he knew that spending time with a space family would be a pretty cool thing to do."

"If he smiled," said Naomi, "maybe he thought we'd be safe. But how would he have known that?"

"I don't know," I said, "Besides asking me a couple of questions about the only thing he did was look at the flowers with his magnifying glass. Maybe they told him something."

"Maybe," said Naomi, "but I doubt it. About the only thing I *am* sure of is that tonight has become even more important than it was before. Tonight we need to find out what they want and decide if it's vital to us."

"Mom, sorry to have to ask you this again," Clayton said, "but what does the word 'vital' mean?"

"Clayton," Naomi said, "'vital' means that something is so important that if you don't have it you'll die. Like aqua vitae is vital to the Browns and learning what the Browns are after could be vital to us."

"BUT MOM," Sam said confidently, "DON'T YOU REMEMBER THAT GRANDPA BOB TOLD US THAT WHEN THE BROWNS FIRST GOT HERE THEY LOOKED FOR AQUA VITAE AND DIDN'T FIND ANY? IF THEY DIDN'T FIND ANY THAT MEANS WE DON'T HAVE WHAT THEY WANT AND THAT MEANS WE'RE SAFE!"

"Bob, is that what George told you?" Naomi asked. "I don't recall you saying that."

"Yeah, Naomi, Sam's right," I said, "but don't feel bad, I'd forgotten it, too. Last night at the Alpine Lounge George said that his family had come here looking for aqua vitae but hadn't found it. In fact, none of the families had found aqua vitae on any of the planets they'd been sent to. So, if we don't have what they want then we probably don't have anything to worry about. I hope that's true, because they seem like such nice people."

"Bob," Naomi answered sharply, "you're welcome to your own opinion of the Browns, but who knows? Maybe they're just good liars. Tonight we'll decide for ourselves if they can be trusted."

"Bob," said Caroline, "Mr. Bond told you that if we found there was a conflict between the Browns' interests and our own, we were to contact him. How were we supposed to do that?"

I pulled out my wallet and extracted the business card that Mr. Bond had given me. I handed it to Caroline, who read it and passed it to Naomi, who read it and passed it to Clayton, who read it and passed it to Sam, who read it and passed it to Mattie, who looked at it and handed it back to me.

"That's awesome!" Clayton said, a look of wonder on his face. "Mr. Bond is Chief Investigator for the Bureau of Extraterrestrial Affairs!"

"THE BUREAU OF EXTRATERRESTRIAL AFFAIRS!" said Sam blissfully, "THAT'S SO COOL!"

"Yep," said Caroline, smiling, "Mr. Bond is the man from BETA."

15

Preparing For Dinner

The rest of the day leading up to our dinner with the Browns was a mixture of awe, fear, excitement, and hard work. Never having hosted a dinner for extra-terrestrials before, Naomi was concerned about the menu. If all the Browns were going to eat was snow cones and bottled water then the rest of us could get by with one of our typical dinners. If, however, the Browns were able to eat regular food, then tonight's meal would require more thought. After fretting over this for a while, she decided that the only way to know was to ask. So after lunch she marched out the front door, pen and paper in hand. She returned minutes later, a dreamy smile on her face.

"I can't believe it," she said several times before finally adding, "She was so nice."

"Naomi," I said, "that's exactly what I've been saying about George and you thought I was crazy."

"So, what can they eat," said Caroline, who was to be assistant chef for tonight's dinner, "I'm dying to know."

The room was suddenly quiet.

"DYING TO KNOW?" Sam called from the living room where he was dusting, "YOU KNOW, GRANDMA CAROLINE, THAT MOM TOLD US NOT TO TALK ABOUT GETTING VAPORIZED!"

Caroline laughed. "Sorry, Sam, then I'll rephrase my question. 'Naomi, I can't wait to hear what they can and can't eat.'"

"Samuel," Naomi warned, "one more vaporizing joke and you're going to your room! Sorry, Caroline. Well, she said they could eat anything. In fact, she said they really like our food. They just have to supplement whatever they eat with their own special stuff, you know, the snow cones. She told me to fix whatever I wanted and she was sure they'd love it…and…" once again Naomi's eyes lost focus, "and she was so nice."

"SORRY, MOM," Sam called from the living room, "BUT IF WE HEAR 'SHE WAS SO NICE' ONE MORE TIME WE'LL HAVE TO SEND YOU TO YOUR ROOM."

Laughing, Naomi said, "OK, Sam, I'll stop saying it….but she was."

"Well," I said, "it must be a huge relief to know that you can fix them whatever you want without being afraid it might kill them."

"Naomi," Caroline said, "I just had a terrific idea about dinner. In fact, it's one of my best ever. We can talk about it and if you think we should do it, there's still enough time."

Clayton walked through the room pushing the vacuum cleaner. "Mom," he said, "I'm going to start vacuuming in the living room and you know how loud this vacuum cleaner is. So, if you and Grandma Caroline need to talk you should probably do it outside."

So, as the vacuum roared, Naomi and Caroline had a short conversation on the deck then came back inside and got ready to go shopping in Sisters.

They hurried out the front door and I was left in charge of Mattie. We went out on the deck and she sat on my lap while I read her stories. Then I took her upstairs for a nap. As I was readying her for bed, she told me she already knew she was going to like the Browns because they were so nice.

I stayed upstairs until she fell asleep then came down and helped the boys finish the cleaning. Naomi and Caroline returned carrying sacks of groceries and disappeared into the kitchen. The kitchen was too small for a third helper, especially a large one like me, so I sat on the couch and read. Then the boys and I went outside and I played goalie while they scored repeatedly over my feeble defense. By then it was getting hot. I came back inside and the boys soon joined me, playing video games while I read.

Naomi ordered the boys to their room for a rest and I went upstairs to lie down and read some more. The Browns were coming at seven, so after a while I got up, shaved and showered again, and when I came back into the bedroom Caroline was there, picking out her clothes for the evening. The smells coming up from downstairs were wonderful. Though I couldn't identify the foods, I could tell by the expression on Caroline's face that this was going to be a very special dinner.

At six forty-five everyone gathered in the dining room. We looked better than I could ever remember us looking during any of our previous trips to Mountainview. Usually it was jeans, shorts, T-shirts, and flip-flops, but not tonight. Then, after what felt like an eternity, there was a knock on the front door and Naomi went to answer it.

16

Dinner With The Browns

The Browns looked as nervous as we felt. George held out a bottle of wine and I took it, thanking him. We shook hands and I said we were glad that they were here. Linda hugged Naomi and Caroline and told them how nice it was to finally meet our family and to be invited to our home for dinner. Naomi introduced the kids to Linda and George and Linda introduced Charles to the adults, then to the boys and Mattie.

Charles waved hi to Mattie and bumped fists with the boys.

Then Clayton said, "I don't know if you remember me but I was at the game place yesterday when you came in and I just want to say, Dude, that you were awesome. I was so impressed."

In a small voice Charles answered, "Thanks, and I do remember you. It was the first time I'd seen you there. I go almost every day. I really love that place."

"You were so good, Dude," said Clayton. "Did it take long to learn to play like that?"

"It took me a while to figure out some of the games," Charles said, his voice getting a little stronger, "but my mom only lets me go there for an hour a day. I think I could be really good if I could stay longer. There are a couple of the games I still have trouble with, but if you'd like to go with me some time I could show you how I play the others. Most of them aren't that hard but they're still fun."

Clayton looked up at Naomi, "Mom, Charles said he would show us how to play some of the games at the arcade if you'd let us go there. That would be so cool."

Naomi smiled and said, "Yes, I heard him." She laughed. "Maybe if you were with Charles it would be okay, but just for an hour a day. I think that's a good rule. You and Sam could use your golf ball money."

I thought all this was beginning to sound a little artificial. So far, tonight was unfolding like any other night when families with grandparents and kids got together for dinner. There hadn't been the slightest mention of anything extra-terrestrial. In a way that was good, but at some point it would need to be addressed.

Then I noticed Sam, who hadn't said a word since the Browns had arrived. He was standing a few feet back from the group, looking up at George and Linda Brown, his mouth open, his eyes glassy. Then George saw him and soon all eyes were on poor Sam, who was locked in a state of awestruck paralysis.

"Sam," Naomi asked, "Are you okay?"

When Sam didn't answer, she went to his side and put her arm around his shoulders, but his expression didn't change.

Then George began speaking. "Sam, I want you to know how happy we are to finally meet you, your mom, and your brother and sister. We've often seen you boys and your sister playing soccer and hunting for golf balls and just as often we've said how nice it would be to meet you. But until yesterday, when your grandfather and I played golf, we hadn't solved the riddle of how to do that."

Slowly George bent his knees until he and Sam were at eye level.

"Although we come from different places we're really very much the same as you, and once you get to know us, you'll find that we're harmless and have no interest in hurting anyone. In fact," he said, smiling, "we don't even have any ray guns."

With that, a tiny smile developed at the corners of Sam's mouth. "No ray guns?" he said softly, "What about laser guns?"

"Not a one," George answered. "I'm sure you're very disappointed in us. Do you think we should bring a few the next time we visit Earth?"

"Yes," Sam said quietly, his smile growing, "if you could bring some for us, too."

"What kind do you think we should bring," George asked, "the kind that tickle you and make you laugh or the kind that vaporize you?"

"The kind that tickle you," Sam answered, looking much more comfortable, "but sometimes I'd like to vaporize Clayton."

Then suddenly Caroline was standing there holding a tray filled with glasses of different sizes.

"There's Champagne in the big glasses for the adults," she said, "and sparkling cider in the little glasses for the kids. Please take a glass and we'll have a toast."

Everyone took a glass and raised it, the kids following the adults' lead. Then Naomi said, "To friendship, wherever you may find it."

"TO FRIENDSHIP," we all answered and clinked glasses.

With that, I felt something warm and wet running down my cheeks. Caroline was right there holding a paper napkin out to me.

"I thought that might happen," she said, "Bob can get pretty emotional in situations like this."

"Yeah," I said, wiping my eyes, "She's right. Sorry," but when I looked around the other adults were reaching for napkins, too.

"Come on, Charles," Clayton said, "I'll show you our games. Some are pretty tough but I bet you can figure them out."

The kids broke away and ran into the living room where the computer games were kept. They settled on the couch and Mattie took her place next to Charles.

Linda Brown disappeared into the kitchen with Naomi and Caroline. I poured George another glass of Champagne and we sat down in the easy chairs opposite the kids.

"George," I said, "thanks for talking to Sam. You did it beautifully. I'm sure he was just overwhelmed knowing where you and your family were from. I was expecting more of a reaction to your arrival than there was, but Clayton had already seen Charles at the arcade so video games were on his mind, and I'm sure that Mattie doesn't understand what being from another planet means. She just thinks you're nice. But I'd like your thoughts on something. Do you think that tonight is some kind of historic occasion, our families getting together like this for dinner?

George, a startled expression on his face, said, "I'm surprised to hear you say that, Bob. As comfortable as you seem with all this, I thought you probably had dinner with extra-terrestrials all the time."

"Well," I laughed, "I always enjoy playing golf with them, but dinner is a new experience."

"Actually, that's a very good question," he said. "Since we're the first people from our planet to come here, our dinner tonight is definitely a first, but I don't know if your planet has been visited before or not."

"That question," I said, "is still being debated. There was a famous incident in Roswell, New Mexico back in nineteen forty-seven that many people believe involved the crash of an alien space-craft. Those same people think that there were beings on-board who either died in the crash or were captured by the military, but our government has always denied both versions. The truth isn't known, but whatever it is, Roswell and visitors from other planets are still hot topics after all these years."

"But," I added, "even if we have been visited before I'm betting that there's never been a situation quite like this."

"You may be right and if so, then here's to us," he said, holding out his Champagne glass for another clink.

"Since we first began thinking you might be from another planet," I said, "there's something I've been curious about."

"Well, you know my policy," said George, smiling. "Ask me anything."

"How did you and your family get so Americanized? With a few minor exceptions you and your family look and act perfectly

American. Even your English is flawless. How did you master all that?

"Well," George answered, "I'm glad we seem authentic to you. Before we got here we were worried that we would immediately be recognized as three aliens from outer space, but instead, we found that we had been very well prepared.

"Our training was extensive," George continued. "Many years of research and practice went into making us look, act, and sound like modern Americans. You don't know this, but for some time we've had drones in your outer atmosphere gathering information about your planet. That's how we've kept up with your speech patterns, slang, current events, and even your fashions.

"And because our planet is nearly 14 light years* from yours it took us a while to get here. In fact, Charles was only three when we left home. Linda and I use our native language around him as little as possible, so English is the only language he knows. Basically, the answer to your question is that we've been well prepared and we've had a lot of time to practice. In fact, I can tell you something funny."

"Good," I said, "I'd like to hear it."

"One of the reasons why Oregon was chosen for our placement was because we kept seeing bumper stickers that said 'Keep Portland Weird,' and we thought that if there were any flaws in our impersonation of Americans, it would be best to be where weirdness was accepted."

---

* A little more than 82 trillion miles

We were still laughing when Caroline came into the room and announced that dinner was ready. The kids were watching Charles play a game on their iPad. George and I stood, getting their attention.

We all trooped into the dining room to discover the lights dimmed and the table lit by three long candles. We marveled at the feast before us. Plates and dishes were piled high with roast turkey, mashed potatoes and gravy, stuffing, green beans, cranberry sauce, and biscuits. Naomi tapped her glass for attention.

"Well, I'm sorry," she said, standing, "that my husband, Tris, couldn't be here for this very special occasion. Unfortunately, he had to work." Then she laughed. "Of course that means more food for the rest of us, but he would have loved to have been here.

"I'd like to begin by saying that we are so honored to have the Browns with us this evening for this special and traditional American Thanksgiving Day dinner."

She glanced at a small piece of paper in the palm of her hand and continued.

"To realize the full meaning of this meal, I need to give you all a brief history lesson. Historians tell us that in 1621 a group of American settlers called the Pilgrims invited a number of the local Indians to attend a dinner they had prepared using food the Indians had given them. The purpose of that dinner was to thank the Indians for their willingness to share both their food and their land with the new settlers. That is the origin of Thanksgiving, one of our most important holidays.

"This year, the real Thanksgiving won't be until November 27th, and of course we're not Indians and the Browns aren't Pilgrims, but despite those shortcomings we think that tonight's dinner still captures the spirit of that occasion. So, I'd like to propose another toast—and this time you'll have to use your water glasses because I forgot to open the wine—to our planet's most recent settlers and our newest friends, the Browns." And once again we lifted our glasses and touched them all around.

During dinner, Sam asked George when the Browns were going to eat their snow cones. When George said that they'd eaten them before leaving home, both Clayton and Sam voiced their disappointment. I explained to the Browns that our family found their snow cones especially fascinating and George promised that at the very next opportunity the kids would have snow cones—minus the aqua vitae—with the Browns.

After the main course the dishes were cleared and everyone was served generous slices of pumpkin or pecan pie slathered with ice cream. Coffee was poured and the cups refilled until there were no more takers.

The evening had been magical. The food, the companionship, and the significance of the evening had combined to produce a unique and unforgettable event.

Then George tapped his water glass and stood.

"When Linda and I were first told that we were to be part of an experiment that involved living on other planets," he said, "we worried about the reception we might receive. The reason for our concern was the tendency of native people to resist the arrival of newcomers, especially if those newcomers were somehow different. For outsiders like us, the key to survival would be the tolerance of the existing people and that was why our leaders chose the United States of America and the state of Oregon. And that was also why we chose to meet your family. And tonight proves the wisdom of those choices."

Then George paused and began again, this time in a more serious manner. "Yesterday, after Bob and I had finished our golf, I told Bob that we might need your help. As I am sure he has told you, problems back home threaten our ability to get more of the substance that landed in your back yard three nights ago.

Last night I told Bob that we would soon be hearing whether we would be allowed to stay in Oregon or would be told to return home. This morning we learned that we must return home. The exact time for our departure has not been set, but it will be within the next two or three days. That means that of the three of us only Charles will make the trip as he is. Linda and I will not be able to do so. That makes us very sad, but there is no other way."

"You don't have to die do you?" Clayton asked, genuine anguish in his voice.

"No, Clayton," George replied, smiling. "Not at all. We have a procedure that we can use to change our bodies back into their component elements so that we can be reformed at a later time. It's not the same as death. In that basic state, we can be restored to be no different than we are right now."

"Is it scary, changing back and forth like that?" Sam asked.

"Not a bit," George said, "although that wasn't always the case. When the procedure was first developed there were some problems, but since then our scientists have improved it to the point that it is very safe. Linda and I will be changed to come back later but Charles will stay as he is. He will make contact with the ship and then the three of us, Linda and I in our condensed forms, and Charles as he is now, will fly back to our home planet. When the aqua vitae we received two nights ago is added to the aqua vitae already on board there will be enough for Charles and the pilot to make the trip."

"A SHIP?" said Sam in amazement. "DO YOU MEAN A SPACESHIP WILL BE COMING TO GET YOU?

Smiling, George said, "Yes, Sam, a spaceship will be taking us home."

Sam was speechless.

"Will we get to see it, the spaceship I mean?" asked Clayton.

"It's possible," said George, "You might even get to ride in it."

The boys looked stunned.

"George," I said, "how will you get the aqua vitae to your spaceship?"

"Once we know when and where the spaceship will be meeting us," he said, "Charles will contact FedEx and have the remaining aqua vitae shipped to that location."

"You mean FedEx will deliver the aqua vitae to your pick-up spot?" I said, amazed.

"Yes," he said with a sly smile, "FedEx is a great company. For enough money they will deliver anything, anywhere, anytime."

I sat there in silence imagining a FedEx driver delivering the Brown's biological container to their spaceship.

"That's amazing," I said, "Do you know where the pick-up will be?"

"No, not yet," he said, "but Charles will be told in a few days."

Then George paused to take a deep breath. "Charles will need assistance with the final preparations and then the three of us will need to be taken to the meeting spot. If you agree to help us, those will be your only responsibilities." He paused again, looking around the table. "So, my question is: will you help us?"

All the Davises enthusiastically nodded their approval.

"Of course we will," I said. "We'll be sad to see you go, but our duties don't sound that difficult."

George was overcome with emotion. "Thank you" he said. "We were hoping you would say yes but we didn't know. It's a great relief. You're all very kind."

"When will you and Linda be going through your conversion procedures?" I asked.

"Tomorrow," he said. "Bob, since you and Caroline are both medical people it might be interesting for you to attend the procedures. We will be starting at eleven o'clock tomorrow morning. If you would like to be present, you are certainly welcome."

Then George looked about the table and said, "Thank you all for a wonderful evening, but we must leave to prepare for tomorrow. And again, thank you for agreeing to help us."

We said our goodbyes and the Browns left.

17

The Procedures

Caroline and I set the alarm so we would be up in time to watch the amazing procedures we had heard about at dinner. We felt very fortunate to have been invited to see them, but at the same time a bit guilty that the rest of the family hadn't. So, before going to bed we had talked to the other Davises and were relieved to find out that with the exception of Sam, they were perfectly satisfied just hearing our descriptions of the procedures.

Next morning Naomi fixed a light breakfast, perfect after last night's feast. Caroline and I hung around for a while then went upstairs, showered, and changed into clean clothes, and around ten forty-five walked up the boardwalk to number sixty-eight. A large wooden crate, most likely destined for FedEx, sat outside their house.

Charles met us at the door and said that his parents were already getting ready. We followed him down a hallway and into a room with a rectangular glass panel in the wall through which we could see George and Linda in the adjacent room, preparing for their conversion procedures. It was a strange sight.

George and Linda's bodies were coated with a clear, glistening oil and the room was filled with an intense greenish-blue light. Charles said that the light and the body coatings were to assure that everything would be clean for the procedures.

Then George moved to a large table covered with white paper and lay down on its top. Next, Linda stepped to the table and applied fifteen or twenty small white squares evenly over his body, each square with a small metal loop in its center. She then pulled a like number of thin, nearly transparent wires from a round dispenser centered above George's body and attached them to the loops. The wires exerted a slight spring-like traction on the squares without pulling them away from George's skin. The wires' dispenser protruded from a long, thin arm mounted to the back of a white box that bore a number of dials and displays on its face and sat on a small table next to George's head.

Once all the wires had been attached, Linda touched a switch on the box and stepped away from the table. Within a few minutes the room's greenish-blue light had gradually changed to mustard yellow as George's skin became increasingly red. I looked at George's face and he appeared comfortable, his breathing still slow and regular even as his skin became redder and redder. I glanced at Linda and she, too, appeared unconcerned about what was happening to George. As the red glow intensified, George began to look less defined, like the picture of a man going slowly out of focus, until he disintegrated into a fine, powdery dust. As this happened the squares detached themselves from his skin and the wires were pulled gently back into the circular dispenser.

When the procedure was over and George was no more than the silhouette of a man made of dust, Linda moved to the table holding a bottle in her hand and sprayed a fine mist over his remains. Then Linda put the bottle down and rolled up the paper on which George rested, inserting it into a cylindrical container and locking its lid in place.

I looked at Charles, and he, too, appeared untroubled by what had just happened to his father. When the light in the procedure room had turned back to greenish-blue, Charles removed his clothes and entered the room where his mother helped coat him with the same shiny substance that had been on both his parents. Then Linda went to the procedure table and lay down and Charles applied the white squares to her skin in the same careful manner that she had done with George.

Once the squares were fastened to the wires, Charles touched the box's switch and the room's color changed to yellow as Linda became increasingly red until she, too, was no more than a dusty silhouette. Then Charles applied the spray, rolled the paper up and sealed it in a metal cylinder identical to George's.

Charles turned off the machine, stored the spray bottle, turned off the lights, and joined us in the observation room, where he dressed quietly. Though he had appeared emotionless during the procedures, he now became tearful.

Caroline hugged him and said, "Charles, you did that so beautifully, but it must have been very hard."

"Thanks," he sighed, wiping away his tears. "I've seen it and practiced it many times, but this was the first time I've actually done it. I'm glad it's over."

"Charles," I said, "why don't you lock up your condo and come back with us to ours? I know Mattie and the boys are anxious to see you and you can stay at our house until it's time to leave."

"That would be great," he said, "but first I need to fix a snow cone. It'll just take a minute."

We walked out of the observation room, Charles closed the door behind us, and we followed him into the dining area.

"Charles," said Caroline, "would you mind if we watched you make your snow cone? We've heard so much about them it would be a treat to see you do it."

"Sure," he said, "No problem."

Like ours, their kitchen was very small, so we watched from the doorway as he made his cone. Their snow cone maker produced a perfect ball of ice and dropped it gently into a paper cup. Then Charles took a bag of aqua vitae from the refrigerator and placed it on the counter. Its contents were still moving, though more slowly than when we had seen them outside. He made a small slit on the top of the bag and inserted a glass tube through which he removed a measured amount of liquid, dripping it evenly over the ice. Charles then put a clip over the hole he'd just made in the bag's skin. He added red flavoring to the snow cone and began eating it.

"As you can see," he said between bites, "it's really pretty simple. In a minute the hole will seal so the container can be used again without fear of contamination. We usually get four or five uses—about a day's worth—out of each packet."

"We saw the crate outside," I said. "How many bags of aqua vitae will you have once it's gone?"

"Counting the one I just opened, I'll have four bags," He said, "That should be plenty."

"But that's only enough for three days after today," I said. "What if you haven't been picked up by then?"

"If that happened," he said smiling, "then you'd need to do the same thing to me that I just did to my mom. It's a little harder than making a snow cone, but not much. You'd do fine. I'd coach you through it, at least until the last part."

Charles finished his snow cone and dropped its paper holder into a wastebasket. He removed the clip he'd just placed on the container and I saw no sign of the original cut. He put the bag back in the fridge and closed the door.

"If we did the procedure on you, Charles, then would we take you and your parents to the spaceship?" Caroline asked, a note of concern in her voice.

"Yes," he said with a reassuring smile, "but don't worry, it won't come to that. I'll be picked up before that's necessary."

"How will you know when that will be?" I asked.

"Each of the relocated families has its own service ship and each ship is able to communicate with us, with each other, and with our home planet," he said. "Would you like to see our communication module? It has a long name but we just call it the communicator."

"Of course," said Caroline, "we'd love to see it."

Charles took us upstairs to a large room where several futuristic-looking devices were positioned around the back of a long curved desk.

"Amazing," I said, looking at the startling assortment of technology. "Which one is the communicator?"

"It's the one in the middle," he said. "I'll call our ship to see if there's any news about when he might be picking me up."

Charles adjusted a dial and pressed two or three buttons and a series of unusual sounds in the rhythm of human speech came through speakers located at both ends of the desk.

"Sorry," he said, "but our pilot's talking to someone in our native language. I'm sure it sounds strange to you. It does to me, too. But Manny—he's our pilot—knows we're waiting. He'll talk to us when he's ready. In the meantime I'll turn on the language converter so we can hear him in English. The converter's the little box to the left of the communicator."

He flipped a switch on the language converter and the meaningless sounds we'd just been hearing were suddenly transformed into perfect English.

"That's amazing," I said, marveling at the seamless transition between the two languages.

A man was talking to a woman. The man told the woman that Charles was waiting so he'd call her later and the two said their good-byes.

Then the man's voice said, "Hello, Charles, I am sorry that I wasn't available when you called but I was talking to my girlfriend. If you turn the language converter off I will talk to you in English."

"Manny speaks English, too," Charles said to us as he flipped the converter's switch.

"Hi, Manny," said Charles, "how are you?"

"Fine, man, fine. My girlfriend still loves me, it's nice and quiet up here today, and I've got a bunch of good movies lined up for later this afternoon."

"I'm sorry to interrupt you, Manny," said Charles, "but I'm at our house and thought I'd check in with you before going back to the Davises'. Have you heard anything yet?"

"Don't worry about it, little dude, if it wasn't for you I'd probably be homeless. No, I haven't heard a thing, but it shouldn't be too much longer. So, how's it goin' down there with you? I hate to ask you this, but have your folks been converted yet?"

"I'm okay," Charles said, "and yes, we did it this morning."

"Man," said Manny sadly, "I'm so sorry. That was your first, wasn't it?"

"Thanks, Manny," Charles said, "Yes, it was my first and it was very hard, but I'm okay now. Listen, Manny, I have some friends with me I'd like you to meet. Their names are Bob and Caroline. Their family will be helping me until we hear something definite, then they'll be taking me to meet you."

"Hi, folks, how ya doin'?" Manny said, "Pleased to meet cha. What do you think of my little buddy there? Pretty cool kid, don't you think?"

"Hi, Manny, this is Caroline. It's so nice to meet you. Yes, we love Charles and he's become such a good friend to our grandchildren. In fact, we've enjoyed knowing all the Browns. Last night our families met for the very first time. We had dinner together and it was such a wonderful evening. We'll be so sad to see them go."

"The Browns are the best, aren't they?" Manny said. "So, you had dinner together last night, huh? Well, I hope it turned out better than what happened in that movie, 'Guess Who's Coming To Dinner' that I was watchin' the other night."

"Manny, I'm so surprised you saw that old movie." Caroline said, "You seem to know an awful lot about our culture. You even sound like one of us. No, our dinner turned out much better than the dinner in the movie. I think we're much more tolerant than Spencer Tracy and Katherine Hepburn were, but of course they lived during a different time. Things have changed a lot since then.

Manny, you may be interested to know that last night, in honor of the occasion, we prepared a meal just like what we serve at Thanksgiving."

"Turkey and all the trimmin's, huh? Wish I could have been there. Maybe sometime though."

Manny had such an amazing grasp of our culture I thought I'd ask him something. "Hey, Manny," I said, laughing, "This is Bob, and it's really nice meeting you. Listening to you talk, it occurred to me that you might be interested in sitting in with our band some night."

"Awe, man," said Manny, "You guys have a band? I'm jealous. What's the name of your band and what do you play?"

"Our band's called RefluxX, with two Xs and I play drums. We're nothing to rave about; just a bunch of old guys having fun."

"Oh, man, I envy you," he said. "You know flyin' around up here with nothin' much to do I spend way too much time listenin' to your music and watchin' your movies and TV. But I just love your culture, man. And your music? I'm a super-big fan of your music, especially Psy, though I guess he's Korean. Sometimes I just put the ship on hover, crank up some Psy, and dance Gangnam style. I'm sure it looks sort of crazy—me dancin' alone in this big ship—but I guess it's whatever floats your boat, and Psy floats mine. Have you guys seen Charles do the dance?"

I was surprised. "No we haven't," I said. "If Charles can dance Gangnam style then he's been holding out on us." I glanced over at Charles, who was blushing and shaking his head. "I hope we can see him dance before he goes. Our grandkids can do it pretty well. Maybe we'll all do it together. Sort of an interplanetary thing."

"Well," said Manny, laughing, "That little dude can really do it. You'll be surprised. You know it's funny, our people have all this technology and go all these crazy places, but in general, man, we're a pretty serious bunch. But then we've had all this trouble with Twin Two and the aqua vitae thing; I'm sure George filled you in on all of that. But for whatever reason, you guys have way more fun than we do. So I've enjoyed my assignment here, gettin' to know more about you Americans. Once I'm back home I'm going to start a band and open a store that sells movies and music from around the galaxy."

"Bringing people together, great idea, Manny," I said, "good luck with that. But if you ever make it to Portland on a Monday night, give me a call and you can meet the band. It's been fun talking to you, Manny, we'll see you in a few days. I'll turn you back over to Charles."

"Thanks, Manny," Charles said. "I'll still be talking to you every day, but I'll be staying with the Davises so it may be less often than it was before."

"That's cool. Thanks, little guy, just call when you can. Nice meetin' you folks. See you soon."

Switching off the communicator Charles said, "Isn't Manny nice? He's a great pilot and he's my best friend. In fact, until yesterday he was my only friend. Except for the first three years of my life—and I don't remember much of that—I've only known three people. So not seeing Manny for two months has been hard, almost as hard as being around people I don't know. I bet I seemed pretty shy when you first saw me last night."

"Maybe a little," said Caroline, "but you weren't too bad. Your parents are out-going and of course Manny is very friendly. I've known a lot of kids much shyer that you, but you did exceptionally well for having been around only three people before coming here."

"That's good," he said. "I was hoping I wouldn't look too uncomfortable. Is there anything else you'd like to see before we go?"

The large machine to the right of the communicator had caught my eye. It was open at the top and bottom and on the floor of its lower opening was a broad conveyer belt. I pointed to it. "That thing looks interesting. What does it do?" I asked.

"We call that the synthesizer. It's another clever machine. It can copy almost anything. Like when we first came here we had no money, but once we got ahold of a few dollars the synthesizer was able to copy them perfectly: dirt, wrinkles and all. I probably shouldn't have told you that," he said, "but we didn't have jobs and you can't live here without money. I hope you don't turn me in to the police."

"No," I laughed, "I'll let you off with a warning this time."

"Thanks," he said, smiling. "And of course the synthesizer made the flowers we planted behind your backyard."

"Maybe you know this," I said, "but parts of the flowers weren't copied by the machine. Caroline and Sam figured that out."

"And," said Caroline, "The longer roots of the new plants were chopped off."

"Yes, I know. Sam and I talked about that last night. When we made the flowers we knew that the smaller parts wouldn't be perfect and that the longer roots would be flattened on the end, but we thought they still might fool you," he said, smiling, "but of course we were wrong. My parents said that the bigger machines back home could have copied the flowers perfectly, but the smaller machines, like this one, have trouble reproducing things that are too big, too small, or too complex, and a flower is a very complicated thing. Is there anything else you'd like to know about?"

Caroline pointed to a large, flat, circular object sitting in the corner of the room. It had a pair of handles and was supported by three wheels. "I'm curious about that, Charles. What does it do?" she asked.

"That's another interesting machine," Charles said. "It's called a gravitational neutralizer and it's what we used to move the biological container back here without causing a huge mess along the way. You put the flat plate over whatever it is you want to lift, then turn it on and the object will float away from the ground so you can move it wherever you want."

"How interesting," Caroline said, looking at me. "That answers a question we've had since your container disappeared. It's all so fascinating, Charles, but that's all I really need to know right now. Thank you for the tour."

There was nothing else I wanted to know about, either. It was a little overwhelming. Technologically, the Browns' civilization was so far ahead of ours that it would take us a long, long time to catch up, if we ever could.

"No," I said, "I've seen enough, too. Thanks for showing us around, and when they're reformed thank your parents for letting us see their conversions. Those were pretty amazing. So, if you're ready, Charles, we could all go back to our place."

"I'm ready," he said. "Go on outside and I'll lock up."

When we got back to number sixty-four, the kids were, as predicted, overjoyed to see Charles again.

18

Waiting

While we waited for the final word from Manny, the kids had a blast with Charles. Almost immediately, Clayton and Sam wanted to know what things Charles could do better than they could. It turned out that he could do most things better than they could, but that didn't seem to bother them. Charles was such a nice kid; gracious and generous, just as his dad had been when we played golf together, that his exceptional abilities didn't seem to generate any jealousy or ill will. Just admiration. Clayton and Sam referred to Charles' superior talents as his superpowers, and I guess they were.

Mattie loved Charles, too, and wherever Charles and the boys went, Mattie was right behind, and whenever Charles sat down, Mattie was next to him.

It didn't take long for the boys to notice Charles' phenomenal eyesight. The kids had been outside playing soccer; Charles against all three of the Davis kids, and during the match Mattie had unknowingly dropped the sparkly blue sunglasses that Caroline had given her. When the kids came inside after their game, Sam noticed that the sunglasses were missing and asked where they were. She touched the top of her head and the glasses were gone! For several seconds she stood perfectly still, trying to remember where she might have lost them. As soon as she realized that the glasses were probably outside where they had just been playing, she rushed out the door and began running back and forth across the lawn looking for them. But after several minutes of frantic and fruitless searching, she came back inside crying. Charles put his arm around her and told her not to worry, they would find her sunglasses together. Mattie stopped crying immediately. "Okay," she said smiling, as though the glasses had already been found. Her faith in Charles was boundless.

Charles told her to go outside and he would tell her how to find them. Mattie ran to the middle of the back yard and turned back toward the house, awaiting further instruction. Charles stood inside the screened door, his eyes scanning the yard.

After only a few seconds he asked, "Mattie, do you know your right from your left?"

Mattie nodded.

"Okay, Mattie," he said, "Now show me your right hand," and Mattie raised her right hand.

"That's perfect, Mattie, now we're going to find your sunglasses. I want you to turn around and start walking toward the fence and I'll tell you when to stop."

Mattie turned and began walking toward the driving range.

After several steps Charles yelled, "Stop!" and Mattie stopped. "Now, Mattie," he said, "Turn to your right!"

She held up her right hand for reference and turned to the right, looking back at Charles.

"Good job, Mattie," he said. "Now go straight," and Mattie began walking slowly forward, her eyes focused on the ground.

Then Charles called, "Mattie, you should be able to see your sunglasses...keep going...right....NOW!" and Mattie stopped, her eyes searching the grass.

"Here they are!" she called joyfully and bent to retrieve the precious sunglasses.

Clayton and Sam had been watching this with interest and when Mattie yelled that she had found her sunglasses, Clayton called out, "Whoa, Dude, that's amazing!" in complete awe of Charles' newest superpower.

Though Clayton was amazed, it didn't take long for Sam to realize the commercial value of this amazing talent.

"DUDE," he said, "WITH EYESIGHT LIKE THAT YOU COULD BE THE GREATEST GOLF BALL FINDER OF ALL TIME!"

And with that the mighty industry of golf ball reclamation began anew, this time with the most advanced piece of golf ball-finding technology on the planet: Charles. With Charles helping Clayton, Sam, and Mattie the rest of the afternoon, the kids found over five hundred balls by dinnertime, a truly phenomenal achievement.

After eating dinner and packing up all the golf balls, Clayton and Sam said that they would like to see the Brown's amazing technology that they'd heard so much about from Caroline and me. So, I walked the boys up to the Brown's condominium. Once they were inside I went back to number sixty-four and waited for their call.

In addition to the Brown's technology, the boys were anxious to see Charles make and eat one of his special snow cones and just as George had promised, fix snow cones for them.

But that worried me. Having been a boy myself, I thought that Clayton and Sam might be tempted to try Charles' aqua vitae. So I told the boys that under NO circumstances were they to eat or drink any aqua vitae. My reasoning was that although it did wonderful things for Charles, it could still be harmful to us. As I was telling them this for about the hundredth time Clayton said, "Don't worry, Grandpa Bob, we don't want it anyway. It looks like snot." And I guess it did.

When their call finally came, I went back and found Clayton and Sam talking excitedly about all the Brown's cool technologic marvels. When the subject switched to snow cones the boys said that those had been great, too, and Charles had even made a cone to take to Mattie.

During their visit, Charles had talked to Manny and there was still no word about the time and place of the pick-up. Clayton and Sam thought that Manny sounded like a hippie, and though I had no idea how they knew that, they were right. Manny did sound like a hippie.

That night, Charles slept in the boys' bedroom where there were two bunk beds and a third bed that had been built to look like a racecar. Naturally, the racecar was the most desirable of the three beds and the boys gave Charles the honor of sleeping there.

The next morning the boys were up early, dragged all five hundred balls to the golf shop, and collected their money. For his help, Clayton and Sam gave all the money to Charles. Though it was only five dollars, Charles was happier than I had ever seen him. At first I had trouble understanding why those five dollars meant so much to him until I realized that they were the first dollars he had actually earned rather than just copied on the synthesizer, and that made them special.

When Naomi asked Charles how he wanted to spend his money, Charles said that if it wouldn't be too much trouble, he would like to go to the Snow Cap for ice cream. He'd heard from his parents that the Twins had no such thing as ice cream, which Charles had quickly learned to love, and the kids had told him that the Snow Cap made the best ice cream in the world. Naomi said that depriving a boy of the best ice cream in the world was a very serious crime and she would happily take the kids to the Snow Cap for lunch.

They spent the remainder of the morning playing soccer. Although Charles had never played the game before, he was just as phenomenal at it as his dad had been at golf. I asked him how, without ever having played the game could he be that good? He said that before coming here his family had been told that Portland was known as "Soccer City USA," so part of his Americanization consisted of watching soccer matches on the video and learning the various shots, just as his father had done with golf.

Clayton loved soccer and hoped that all the hard work he had put into his game this summer would pay off and he would be drafted up to the minor league Tai Tam Tigers when school started.

He and Charles spent some time together talking strategy and practicing various shots, and when the game of Clayton, Sam, and Mattie versus Charles began again it seemed to me that Clayton was playing even better than he had before.

When one o'clock arrived Naomi took all the kids into Sisters for burgers and cones at the Snow Cap. After returning home, Charles thanked her repeatedly and said that when he got back home he would open Snow Cap Two.

19

The Plan

The kids played video games the rest of the afternoon then Charles went home for a snow cone and a chat with Manny. When he returned he looked dejected and said that Manny had told him that the pickup would be tomorrow night.

My initial reaction was relief that Caroline and I wouldn't have to perform a conversion procedure on him. Although I thought we could probably pull it off, it was worrisome to think that Charles' life might depend on our ability to do something we'd never done before.

But that was no longer an issue and the more I thought about Charles returning home, the worse I felt for him. Besides Manny, we were the only friends he'd ever had and strong bonds had developed. He would miss us just as we would miss him. But it was more than that. By the time Charles got home he'd have spent ten of his thirteen years in space with just three people. Of course, they were three very nice, talented, and interesting people, but living such a limited life had no appeal to me.

"Charles, I'm so sorry you'll be leaving us," said Naomi. "Although it will be nice for you to see your home again, we'll be sad to see you go. You've become a part of our family."

"But," I said, "just think of all the stories you can tell people back home about your experiences here: golf balls and soccer, ice cream and dancing Gangnam style, and…"

"AND," said Sam, "YOU CAN TELL THEM HOW STRANGE AND HORRIBLE WE ARE. LIKE WE'RE THE MOST HIDEOUS CREATURES YOU'VE EVER SEEN."

But once the laughter had disappeared Clayton said, "Seriously, Dude, we'll miss you so much."

During this conversation, Mattie had sidled up to Charles and now wrapped one arm around his back and rested her head against his shoulder, rubbing her other hand against her eyes to keep back the tears.

Then Charles said, "And I'm going to tell my parents they should have more children; two brothers and a sister would be perfect."

Though it was a beautiful thing to say, funny and heartfelt at the same time, my practical side had kicked in and I was already thinking about all the things that would need to be done before Charles left. So, breaking the spell, I said, "Charles, did Manny tell you where and when he'd be picking you up?"

"He said that right behind us, on the other side of the highway, there's a small mountain called Black Butte. Normally there's a fire observer living on top, but Manny's arranged for him to be gone tomorrow night. Although there are lots of hikers there during the day, it's illegal to hike or camp on the mountain at night. He said there's a parking lot about halfway up the mountain and a good trail from there to the top. Manny thought it would take about two hours for us to hike from the parking lot to the summit and that's where he'll meet us, tomorrow at midnight."

"Okay," I said, "Well, now we know, and though I hate to be the first one to say it, we should get busy. I'll get directions to the Black Butte parking lot and find out all I can about the trail. Charles, what will you need to do before you go?"

"A few days ago my dad called our condo's owner and told him we'd probably be leaving by the end of the month. I'll call him and confirm that. Then our rental car has to be returned to the rental agency in Bend and the container needs to be FedEx'd to the Black Butte observer's cabin. Then we'll have to do something with all the stuff that's at our place; store it somewhere. I think that's about it."

"You can leave your things with us," Naomi said. "There's plenty of space in the spare bedroom on the second floor. We never use that room anyway. Hopefully, once your aqua vitae problem is solved you'll come back to Oregon, but if not, we can deal with your stuff then."

I'd been thinking about something that Charles had said when he first told us when he'd be leaving. "Charles, you said that Manny had arranged for the fire observer to be gone tomorrow night. How did he do that?"

"I was curious about that myself," said Charles, smiling, "so I asked him and he said that he'd called the man pretending to be his supervisor and told him he was being transferred to Colorado on an emergency basis. The man will be leaving tomorrow morning. When he gets far enough away, Manny will call him again and explain that it was a false alarm and that he should get back to Black Butte right away. But until he's back Manny will watch for forest fires and call the man's supervisor if he sees one."

"Interesting," I said, chuckling. "Manny's a pretty talented guy, isn't he?"

"Yes," said Charles, nodding his head and smiling, "he's very clever."

"Dude, could we use some of your stuff to talk to you after you leave?" Sam asked Charles. "Would the communicator work while you're traveling and then when you get back home?

I knew that super-scientist Sam would love to use the Brown's cool technology when Charles was gone, and if it could be used to stay in touch with Charles that would make everyone happy.

"I'm sure it would," Charles said. "And it's easy to use. I can show you guys how to work it, and some of the other things, too. Once I get home you'll be reaching me through people who don't speak English, so you'll need to know how to work the language converter, too."

"THAT WOULD BE SO COOL," said Sam happily.

We spent the rest of the afternoon and evening carrying the equipment from the Brown's condo over to the bedroom on the second floor. We collapsed and stored the room's twin beds then set up the curved desk and all the electronics just like they'd been in Charles' condo. Then we packed all the conversion equipment into the storage shed next to the condo and covered it with a tarpaulin, and finally, we carried over the canisters containing Charles' parents, the snow cone maker, and the three remaining bags of aqua vitae.

In preparation for what was sure to be a busy day tomorrow, Mattie and the boys went to bed early. I stayed up with Caroline and Naomi, and used Caroline's laptop to get more information about the Black Butte trail, which we would be hiking in the dark twenty-four hours from now.

The trail looked straightforward. It began in a heavily forested part of the mountain, but midway the trail emerged from the trees and was open the rest of the way. The hike's degree of difficulty was described as either "moderate" or "moderate to hard," the hard part, and the part that I was dreading, was that the trail was steep. We would be gaining over 1600 feet, more than a quarter mile of elevation, in less than two miles.

Though Naomi and the boys would have no trouble getting up the trail, neither Caroline nor I were in very good shape. But I was hoping that the prospect of seeing their spaceship, meeting Manny the hippie pilot and devoted fan of American pop music and Psy, and saying good-bye to Charles would be more than enough incentive to get us to the top.

I told Caroline and Naomi everything I had learned about the trail and we made a list of all the items we would need for the trip. Descriptions of the hike up Black Butte always emphasized how hot it could get during the day and that there was no water available on the trail, but we'd be hiking at night so heat wouldn't be an issue. In fact, hiking in the middle of the night on an open slope at an altitude of 6500 feet would be cold, and we'd need to dress accordingly and carry plenty of snacks. Caroline and I had brought our backpacks from Portland and Naomi said that the boys had packs and that she had an extra pack for Charles as well as a child carrier backpack with which to carry Mattie.

When we had completed our list, we marked everything we would need to get tomorrow and called it a night.

Next morning everyone was up early, ate breakfast, and went about his or her tasks. Caroline drove to Sisters for the additional food and equipment. The boys went to the Browns' condo and collected everything that still needed to be stored and carried it to the Davis's house then went back to strip the beds, wash the sheets, and throw the trash away.

Once I had washed the breakfast dishes and put them away I drove the Brown's rental car into the city of Bend and returned it to the rental company. Then Naomi and Mattie picked me up and took me to the FedEx office where I made arrangements for FedEx to deliver the aqua vitae by helicopter to the observer's cabin on the summit of Black Butte later that afternoon. To my surprise, FedEx didn't bat an eye and it cost even less than I expected. Good company.

When we got home the boys had finished setting up all of the Browns' electronic equipment and Charles was showing Clayton and Sam how to operate it. I went to the Lodge and used their printer to copy maps of the Black Butte trail. Naomi collected everything the kids would need for tonight and put it in the living room so that it would be in one place when it came time to leave. We met in the dining room for lunch then Naomi had the kids lie down to rest. They would need all their energy for tonight.

Dinner was a somber occasion and little was said. We had ice cream sundaes for dessert. It would be the last ice cream that Charles would eat until he got home and started Snow Cap Two, spreading peace and joy throughout the Twins and winning his planet's equivalent of the Nobel Prize.

After dinner we changed into our hiking clothes then checked and readied our gear. Naomi packed the snacks and water bottles while Caroline and I gathered the equipment we would need later tonight. By then it was nine o'clock and time to go. We grabbed our stuff and filed out the door. Everything was loaded into Naomi's van and off we went to live out the final chapter of our great adventure.

20

Black Butte

Leaving the Ranch, we turned right onto Highway 20 and drove two and a half miles toward Sisters then turned left at a sign saying "Indian Ford Campground" onto Green Ridge Road. We stayed on Green Ridge Road for 3.8 miles then turned left onto gravel Road 1110 where we encountered our first problem: Road 1110 was a "washboard" road.

Sometimes a dirt road will develop a wavy, bumpy surface similar to an old-fashioned metal washboard. This can happen when cars bounce repeatedly over an unpaved road's surface. If there's a lot of traffic and the dirt is soft then the bounces will begin to create peaks and valleys and with each additional vehicle the peaks will become sharper and closer together. Driving on a washboard road is like driving on a road covered with speed bumps, and the bumps on Road 1110 were the worst I'd ever experienced.

Naomi tried to maintain a decent speed but it was impossible. As long as she kept the speed at 10 MPH or less the bouncing was tolerable, but above that speed the bouncing and lurching were so extreme it felt like the van would fly apart. Unfortunately, we needed to stay on this road for 5.8 miles and driving that distance so slowly would put us behind schedule. But if the van was going to make the trip in one piece we had no other choice. So, Naomi slowed down, explained the problem to the kids, and asked them to be patient.

It was almost dark when we finally reached the Black Butte visitor's parking lot and encountered problem number two: the forest ranger. Except for the ranger's white USDA Forest Service pick-up the lot was empty, the ranger busy putting padlocks on the bathroom doors.

Once the ranger had finished with the locks, he ambled slowly across the lot to our van. Naomi lowered her window and the ranger bent down, looking suspiciously inside.

Completing his inspection, he drawled, "Well, folks, it looks like you might be planning to hike up the Butte tonight. Sorry, but the trail's closed and there's no camping at night. I'm surprised you didn't know that. It's posted everywhere."

"Sir," said Naomi, a hint of irritation in her voice, "we've read the signs and we're aware of the rules, so you can relax; we're not climbing the mountain tonight. We're here to show the kids what they'll be up against if they try to climb it tomorrow. That way if someone doesn't feel up to it then he or she can back out now rather than when we're halfway to the top."

The ranger paused, considering her words, but looked unconvinced. "Well, ma'am, I guess I've never thought of it quite like that before, but you're right. You start tomorrow and one of the kids decides it's too hard then you'll all have to quit. I get it. But rules are rules and right now everything's closed. So, please head back to the main road and I'm sorry about those bumps."

The ranger stepped back from the window, still eyeing us suspiciously. Naomi nodded, switched on the headlights, turned the van around, and started back down the bumpy road.

"Thanks, Naomi," said Caroline, "that was quick thinking, but now we have a problem. We can't drive back to Green Ridge Road and hike from there, it's too far, and if the ranger sees our van parked anywhere along the dirt road he'll know we're up to something and come looking for us."

"Naomi," I said, "in the next quarter mile there's a road that branches off from this one. I saw it on the way up. It's not very big but it might be enough to hide us until the ranger finishes up and goes back to town."

Then I saw it.

"There it is, Naomi, on the left!" I said, just as we passed a pair of tire tracks disappearing into the heavy brush. Naomi slammed on the brakes and backed up.

"Now listen everyone," she said, "we'll be breaking the law, but this might be our only chance of getting up Black Butte tonight."

"Naomi," I said, "This *is* our only chance. But if we get caught we can call Mr. Bond. I've still got his card."

"You're right," said Naomi, laughing, "I'd forgotten about Mr. Bond."

She put the van back in gear and nosed it into the small opening, branches scraping our sides and top. We drove twenty or thirty feet into the foliage until we could go no farther.

"Not much of a road," I said. "Maybe it's just for turning around."

"Or," said Caroline, "hiding from the ranger when you need to climb Black Butte at night."

"That, too," said Naomi, laughing.

Whatever its purpose, it was exactly what we needed. We sat quietly in the van, listening for the ranger's truck as our cooling engine made pinging sounds.

Minutes passed and I began to grow impatient.

"Maybe," I whispered, "someone should go outside and listen for the ranger's truck and warn us when he's coming."

"Good idea, "Naomi said, "who…"

"Me," said Sam, lowering his window and scrambling out before anyone could react.

He'd been gone only a few seconds when his head reappeared in the window. "Shuuush," he whispered, "He's coming. Everyone be quiet!"

Then we heard the ranger's truck approaching, its tires chattering against the bumpy road and scattering rocks. I closed my eyes, held my breath, and crossed my fingers for good luck.

But our little hiding place didn't attract his attention. The truck's noises grew louder then slowly disappeared down the road.

"Should we just leave the van here?" I asked in a whisper.

"Yes, definitely," Caroline said. "If the ranger didn't believe Naomi's story he might come back later and check the lot."

"Good idea," said Naomi. "And please climb out the windows if you possibly can. The fewer scratches we get on the van the better. And be sure to bring all your stuff!"

Although I was the biggest and oldest person in the group, my exit through the window was surprisingly agile. Caroline also made it out with ease. Re-entry would be another matter, but one we could deal with when the time came.

Once everyone and everything was out of the van, we assembled on the roadway. Naomi checked the kids to make sure they were ready, I lifted Mattie into the child carrier backpack and we started up the dirt road. The forest ranger had added another quarter mile of steep hiking to our trek and when we reached the parking lot it was dark and cold. I glanced at the luminous numbers on my watch. The ranger had also cost us another fifty minutes. It was now ten forty-five and making it to the top by midnight was no longer possible.

On her trip into town Caroline had bought six small, bright LED flashlights attached to elastic headbands. Now, she went around passing them out. We switched the lights on, adjusted their beams, took a final swig of water, and started up the trail.

For the first hour, the dense canopy of trees permitted no more than an occasional glimpse of the sky. The trail was just as steep as I had feared and I was soon breathing hard and walking at the end of the line. Caroline was in front of me, then Sam, then Charles—his parents' canisters poking out from his backpack—then Clayton, and finally Naomi with Mattie on her back.

We climbed another fifteen minutes and suddenly emerged from the trees with the sky in full view. The moon was huge and the sky filled with more stars than I had ever seen. There was so much light coming from the sky that the little flashlight on my headband seemed unnecessary and as I snapped it off I saw everyone in front of me doing the same.

We stood there in respectful silence, stunned by the immensity and magnificence of the universe around us. Surely, I thought, on a few of the planets circling those stars there were beings similar to us, each with their own hopes and dreams, troubles and fears. I could even imagine that somewhere up there another band of hikers was trudging up a mountain to meet a man in a spaceship.

When we resumed our climb, I noticed that if I looked up and to the left I could now see the rounded top of Black Butte, its dark shape outlined against the starry sky. I looked down and saw what were probably the lights of Mountainview Ranch. They were a long way down. Clearly we had gained more altitude than I would have guessed.

The kids were uncomplaining and self-sufficient. They marched tirelessly, talking quietly among themselves. I'm sure there were things they could have complained about but so far I hadn't heard a negative word from anyone.

Even with Mattie on her back Naomi made the climb look effortless, and when we stopped to rest she was always available to give cheerful encouragement to the rest of us.

Caroline, too, was moving well. Preparing for our trek she had repeatedly voiced concerns about her ability to make it to the top, and more than once she had threatened to stay home. But having hiked with her many times, I knew she was always better than her predictions. A few years ago, when we were planning to hike to the bottom of the Grand Canyon and out again, she had voiced similar fears, but then had performed as well or better than I had.

Since leaving the trees it felt like the slope of the trail had increased. It was either that or I was getting tired, but taking example from the rest of the group, I kept my struggles to myself. This was our chance to have the experience of a lifetime and I wasn't going to spoil it for anyone else.

We continued on a straight course for another twenty minutes and then the trail began to curve gradually to the left. Through this section we encountered a number of large rocks on the trail that we stepped between as though we were crossing a stream rock by rock. Here we stopped frequently to catch our breath, take sips of water, and encourage each other with reminders that we were almost there.

Hiking higher, I could now see the dark outline of the lookout tower. My reading had said that the tower was built in 1995 and was used by the observers to watch for forest fires. As we neared the summit, more and more of the tower came into view and the trail seemed to flatten.

My heart was now thumping wildly, both from the effort of the climb and from the prospect of seeing my first spaceship. The trail continued, but on a slight decline as we began moving toward the far side of the butte. If there was a spaceship anywhere near I didn't see it. We were now well past the tower and facing the original cabin, which had been built in the 1920s and was notable for a small square cupola on the peak of its roof. The entire crest of the butte was now visible and there was still no Manny. I checked my watch. It was after one o'clock. Were we too late?

But then we heard it: Dum—Dum—Dum————Dah-Dum*, followed by the banging of timpani and the entire sequence repeating, louder and more intense. Then slowly over the crest of the hill floated a great dark shape. It rose majestically then paused, hovering silently above the butte, and with the third repetition of the music's powerful theme, the lights inside the ship exploded on and we saw the ship's pilot grinning at us from behind his consol. It was Manny.

Manny brought his ship down into a hover between where we were standing and the old cabin. I estimated that the ship was about seventy-five feet long, thirty-five or forty feet wide, and shaped like a giant football. The front portion of the ship was transparent with the console where Manny sat visible in its center. The spaceship certainly wasn't what I'd imagined, but it was still impressive in its simplicity.

Then a large oval door on the side of the ship opened and descended slowly to the ground, and when it stopped a thin handrail rose from its right side.

Manny stepped out of the ship and looked around. He was short with a broad, friendly face and curly red hair. "Nice night, huh? Reminds me of home; a little greener, but not too much different."

Charles ran to Manny and gave him a big hug.

---

* Here you might like to listen to the beginning of "Also Spake Zarathustra" by Richard Strauss, the music Manny was playing for the hikers.

"Glad to see you again, little dude," said Manny, returning the hug. "Hey, why don't you introduce me to your friends? Looks like you're in with a pretty rough crowd."

As always, Mattie was glued to Charles' side. "Manny," Charles said, "This is my friend, Mattie. She's almost three."

"Hi, Mattie," Manny said, "It's nice to meet you." He stepped back to examine her more carefully. "Oh, yeah!" he said, "Aren't you a sweetie. In a few years you'll be driving the boys wild, won't you? Manny squatted and gave Mattie a hug, then stood again.

"And who are these two shady-looking characters?" he said, pointing to Clayton and Sam.

"Manny," Charles said, "This is Clayton and that's his brother, Sam, and they're my best friends... besides Mattie...and you."

"You guys want a hug, a handshake or a fist-bump?" Manny asked. They opted for hugs.

Manny stood and reached for Naomi's hand. "And you must be the mom. Looks like you've done a pretty good job so far, but I'd keep an eye on 'em. Hi, I'm Manny," and their handshake became another hug.

"And this lovely lady," he said looking at Caroline, "I'm guessin' she must have fallen for the drummer. Am I right?"

Caroline laughed and answered, "Manny, you know how it all works, don't you?"

"Well," he answered, smiling, "it works pretty much the same no matter where you go. Pleased to meet cha, kid," he said, hugging her.

"And you," he said eyeing me critically. "Man, it looks like you could use some refreshments. Climbing up here must be a little harder than sitting behind a sweet set of skins on a Monday night. Nice to meet cha, man."

I'd been worried that as the senior member of the group I might just get a fist-bump, but I got a hug, too.

"Well, listen guys," Manny said, "It's a little chilly out here so let's step inside my mobile home and I'll show you around. I've got some snacks and refreshments on board and in a while I'll fly you back to the parkin' lot. Sorry about the ranger, I was watchin' while all that was goin' on, but you guys did just fine. Couldn't have done it better myself. Oh, and in case anyone was wonderin', the aqua vitae arrived on schedule and has already been packed away. So, welcome to the good ship Lenore. That's my girlfriend's name."

Inside, the spaceship was amazingly plain. The walls and ceiling of its rear two-thirds were covered with compartments of various sizes and there were three benches and a few seats attached to a peculiar pebbly floor. In the front, there was only the steering wheel, two levers, and two seats.

"So how does this thing work, Manny?" I asked. "Except for the steering wheel and a couple of levers I don't see how you control or monitor your ship. And what kind of propulsion system do you have? Your ship doesn't make a sound."

"Well," he said, "I can't give you a technical description 'cause I don't understand it all myself, but the ship runs on gravity. Several years ago we figured out how to collect these tiny particles called gravitons and since then those little buggers have been our main source of power.

"Maybe the Browns told you about the set-up back home; how ours is one of two planets that share a moon and circle the sun together?"

I nodded.

"Well that arrangement made us pretty familiar with gravity early on, and so one way or another a lot of our stuff runs on gravity. When the ship gets close to another planet we suck up a bunch of their gravitons in this contraption on the bottom of the ship and then when we want to leave we just reverse the process and off we go. So, as we're flyin' through the galaxy, we sort of hop from planet to planet. It works pretty well, we never run out of gas, and except for the initial cost it's all free. And gravity power doesn't make much noise, either. In fact, it doesn't make any. So, when we're cruisin' around some planet that's not our own, we don't attract much attention. And that's a good thing since a lot of these folks are pretty suspicious, and not very friendly either.

"But as far as monitors go, we've got plenty of those, probably more than we need. Right now you just can't see 'em, but once we get this thing cranked up they'll be pretty obvious."

Then Manny served us food and drinks. Everything tasted great, but none of the foods had much texture and each item was a single color, with red, blue, and green being the most common. But after I'd eaten some of their food and downed a few of their drinks I felt much better. In fact, I felt great. The fatigue I'd experienced earlier had disappeared and I felt like I could go non-stop the rest of the night.

Then Manny turned on some current American music and mixed it up with some stuff from the 60s and 70s, the Beatles, the Stones, and some of the psychedelic stuff, too, and we had ourselves a little party, which, in fact, may have been the best little party I'd ever been to in my entire life. Manny was a terrific host and here we were sitting in a spaceship on the top of Black Butte, under an immense canopy of stars, listening to great music, and being entertained by our new friends from outer space. Really, what more could you want?

When I finally checked my watch it was almost four o'clock, and my earlier prediction that I could go all night without sleep was looking doubtful. I was beginning to fade and as I glanced around, my fellow partygoers were looking a little faded, too.

"Listen, guys," said Manny, "I should get you down to the parkin' lot before the sun comes up and the ranger comes back to open the johns. So, if you'll just hand me your plates and glasses and sit down, I'll ease this thing down the hill. It's been a super night and I'm glad we found some way to thank you for everything you've done for us."

We handed over our plates and glasses and Manny got behind the spaceship's wheel, moved one of the levers, and we began to rise slowly from the top of the butte. And as soon as he had touched the controls, the lights inside the ship dimmed and the transparent nosecone was suddenly ablaze with orange lines and squiggly symbols that were undoubtedly the dials and gauges that I had feared might be missing.

From the console, Manny said, "So, Bob, it turns out there are lots of things to look at after all. And another nice thing about a ship that runs on gravitons is that it makes its own gravity, so when we head off into space we're not floatin' around like your astronauts do. But don't worry, you'll figure it all out soon enough. It's not that much of a jump from what you're doin' now."

The ship glided down the hill and hovered over the gap in the trees above the parking lot then slowly descended until the door opened and the entire pack of weary revelers filed out into the parking lot.

Manny and Charles went around to each of us and thanked us, promising that when things got better they'd be back and we'd have another party. There were hugs all around, we said our good-byes and then turned and began shuffling down the road toward the van.

"Oh, Sam," Charles called from the door of the space ship. We stopped and turned toward his voice, "One more thing. The last packet of aqua vitae is in your refrigerator and as long as you keep it cool it will last indefinitely. Maybe you or someone you know can figure out how to make what's inside, and if you do let us know. It's just a thought, but I know you're interested in stuff like that."

Then Manny appeared behind him. "And listen guys," he said, "The little dude and I have cooked up a surprise for you. So, give us a second to get ready and I'll turn the ship around so you can watch."

They entered the space ship, the door closed, and a few seconds later the ship lifted a few feet off the ground and swung around so that its nose faced us. Then the lights inside the ship flashed on and the parking lot was suddenly filled with loud electronic dance music, and there were Manny and Charles, one on each side of the console, dancing Gangnam Style. Then the Davis kids joined in and finally Naomi, Caroline and I were doing our own lame versions of the dance. Then the ship slowly ascended through the opening in the trees, the music booming and Manny and Charles still dancing. We applauded until the ship was out of sight.

21

Bugs

We got home just as the sun was coming up. I went right to bed and didn't get up until early afternoon. While I was in the bathroom washing and shaving I could hear the boys in the bedroom next door talking to Manny and Charles on the communicator. They sounded very happy.

Well, I'm sure it was great fun for them, but personally I'd had enough of spaceships and aliens and aqua vitae for a while and was looking forward to getting back to normal. I got dressed and went downstairs, fixed some coffee, and looked in the fridge for something to eat.

But when I opened the refrigerator door I saw a plastic container with a piece of notebook paper heavily scotch-taped to its side. The writing on the paper said AK-WA V-TAY, DO NOT EAT OR YOU'LL DIE!!!!! I obeyed the warning and gathered some other things to eat. I had just settled into a dining room chair with my food and today's newspaper spread out in front of me, when the phone rang.

Unhappy for the interruption, I walked into the living room and lifted the phone from its cradle. I answered with a brusque

"Yes!" and after a long pause a male voice said, "Well.... ......how was it?"

It was Mr. Bond.

"Mr. Bond," I said, "how nice of you to call, sir. Now I suppose I could say, 'How was what, Mr. Bond?' but then you'd know I was lying, wouldn't you?"

There was another long pause. "Maybe," he answered.

"Well, our friends have gone home," I said, "So I'll just say that it was one of the greatest experiences of my life and I'm sure the rest of the family feels the same. And I'm also happy to report that they weren't after anything we had. At least nothing that we know about."

Another pause. "Good." he said. "A few of them can be unpleasant but most are quite nice. My men will be coming for the bugs."

"Bugs?" I said just as the line clicked dead. I hung up the phone and as his words were beginning to make sense there was a loud knock at the front door. That's crazy, I thought, that couldn't be Mr. Bond's agents already...could it?

But it was. BETA was clearly a more efficient operation than your average government agency. I opened the door for the two men, their badges again out for my inspection. They entered the house and while the black agent assumed a "rest" position in the middle of the dining room, the white agent motioned for me to follow him, saying I would need to notify anyone still in his or her room that he was there to collect some "government property."

We walked upstairs and I followed him from room to room as he gathered the listening devices. As their name implies, the bugs looked like small black insects and there must have been a dozen or more scattered throughout the house.

On the top floor, Naomi and Mattie were up, dressed, and ready to go downstairs. The only person still asleep was Caroline, who as you know by now is one of the world's greatest sleepers. She was still in bed, the covers pulled over her head.

In a loud voice I said, "Caroline, just stay where you are. One of Mr. Bond's men is here to collect some things they left during their last visit."

From beneath the covers came, "Permission granted."

The agent took a bug from behind a leg of the window seat then moved to the second bedroom, opening the door to find two surprised and guilty-looking boys standing in front of a jaw-dropping array of futuristic technology. The agent entered the room and assessed the situation.

I thought he would order the boys from the room while he and his partner seized the equipment, but instead he just looked at them, nodded once, and removed a bug from the back of a lamp. We then descended the stairs, the other agent joining us in the hallway. I followed them to the front door.

Opening the door, the black agent turned and gave me a small, crooked smile.

"Have a nice day," he said then followed his partner out onto the wooden walkway, the screen door closing quietly behind them.

THE END

Bob Crumpacker is a retired neurologist living in Portland, Oregon. This is his first novel. A second story, "The People In the Cave," will be available soon.

Made in the USA
San Bernardino, CA
25 July 2015